# RABBIT EARZ

by Anthony Scattini

Rabbit Earz
Publisher: Anthony Scattini




Disclaimer:

This book is a work of fiction. Any resemblance to actual persons, living or dead, is purely coincidental. The characters, events, and incidents portrayed in this book are the products of the author's imagination or are used fictitiously.

ISBN  979-8-9943891-0-2

Author & Design: Anthony Scattini

Cover Anthony Scattini

First printed in Plesanton, CA

Who amongst us hasn't experienced their own Rabbit Earz when listening to the absurdities on and around a golf course? Rabbit Earz not only dives into the unexpected bonds we all create on the golf course, but you will swear that you know and have golfed with a similar cast of characters.

So join Zip and Biggs on their hilarious and heartfelt journey that guarantees you'll enjoy this page turning tale while also helping those that live with Multiple Sclerosis.

*" It takes a lot of courage to show your dreams to someone else "*

**Erma Bombeck**

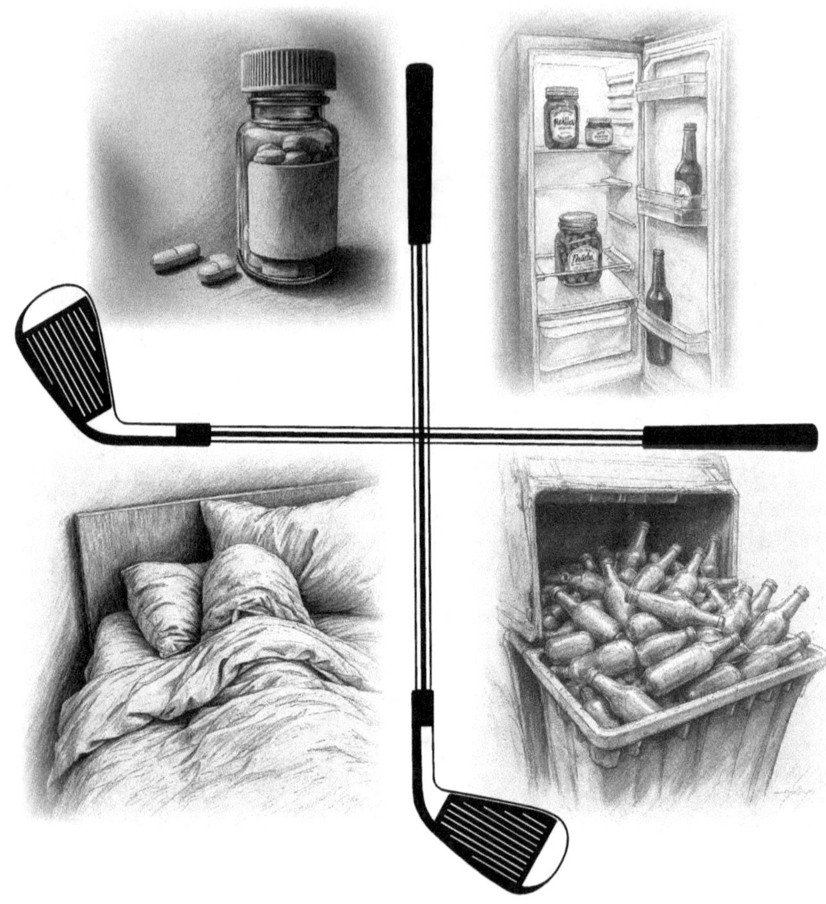

## HOLE #1

"Dad, get UP!"

The routine morning bustle was in full swing. Maggie's pace could easily be heard as the hardwood floors creaked with every frantic footstep. Maggie conceivably raced from her bedroom to the bathroom to the kitchen. Each time she passed her father's bedroom she'd bark out again.

"Dad, get up!"

This cadence she repeated didn't have an alarming tone. It was as repetitive and normal as the sun coming up and the start of a new day. She knew eventually there would be movement. She counted on it. Maggie's father relied on this daily dance as well. He never set an alarm clock. In fact, the sound of an alarm going off was a sound he absolutely dreaded. He flat out hated any type of alarm. An alarm only added to the pain he already felt. The undeniable torture of having to rise again and try to shake off another hangover from a night of solo drinking, smoking, and pill popping. It was a discipline only a professional drinker performed.

This particular morning was another rinse and repeat. A ritual where he passed out the previous night sitting upright on the couch with ESPN blaring on the television. He'd then stammer to the refrigerator and squint at the tiny clock on the microwave next to it that usually read somewhere around 3:00 a.m. He'd slam a few huge tugs off a Gatorade bottle and be grateful that he had roughly four more hours to sleep before he'd hear those creaks and crackles of Maggie's footsteps across the floors as another morning demanded he get his crushed ass out of bed to drive her to school. It wasn't easy. Especially because his discomfort was self-induced. But he managed for years.

Rinse and repeat. Oh, how he wanted Maggie to be sick this morning so he wouldn't need to take her to school. There was the time in the first grade John's hangover was so crushing he decided that his family name was just as important as Washington's, Lincoln's, or MLK's, so out of desperation he created Harrison's Day. He decided the Harrisons deserved a holiday too, just as those iconic historical figures were awarded.

"After all," her dad explained to Maggie, "the Harrisons were just as special as those guys, so why should we have to go to work or school?"

This made perfect sense to a six-year-old and gave John an excuse to go back to bed. So he lied to his daughter. He knew he'd catch hell from her mom, but those mornings were so debilitating he didn't care. He couldn't care. He simply could not shake the pain. But Maggie was not sick today. She took school seriously and would never miss. And, since John had used up his Harrison's Day graces, he knew he needed to drag himself out of bed.

For so many normal folks this notion of not being able to get up seemed absurd. And it was. But John partied hard. And when that discomfort hit him, it hit him HARD. Perhaps harder than most. But most don't pollute themselves with the drugs and alcohol John used. After he heard the customary amount of creaking along the hardwood floors that he was accustomed to, he knew Maggie was about ready. She had crisscrossed the hallway, brushed her teeth, made her lunch in the kitchen, and when John heard the freezer's ice machine fill her water bottle, he knew that was her final task before she passed by his room one last time on the way to the garage.

"Dad, GET UP!" she'd sing one last time.

He pulled the pillow sandwich off his head, sat up and looked at that awful person in the mirror across from his bed. He felt disgusted . . . again.  It was no wonder his bed was long devoid of a mate. How could anyone possibly want to share this bed, this life? John was a middle-aged, rapidly aging, beer- bellied, tortured soul. He couldn't possibly blame Maggie's mom for leaving. But he did have Maggie. His one true joy. He was so grateful for Maggie. She gave him the only bit of purpose he had on this rock. John had fought hard in family court to retain this fatherhood he deserved and he was not going to fuck that up. John knew that, without Maggie, he didn't have a chance. He didn't really care about anything else. His picture was definitely not in the dictionary under exemplary father. John, like many if not all, had his demons.

John extracted himself from his cave of a bedroom and stumbled to his refrigerator whose occupants consisted of cheese, half and half for coffee, spaghetti sauce for Maggie, and a jar of pickles. He prayed he could find one or two remaining cold beers. This morning he was in luck. He popped the top off of what wasn't consumed last night and quickly chugged as much as he could while Maggie laid on their truck's horn from the driveway. She cared very little if the blaring horn disturbed any neighbors. John had a "special cabinet" above the fridge where he kept his vape pen and pills. It was out of Maggie's reach when she was younger, but now that she was 16 he worried she could find his stash. He nervously shook the pill bottle hoping he'd left a few for this morning's hangover and was relieved to hear the rattle of two lonely survivors clang against the plastic.

"Thank God," he murmured to himself, as he threw the pills into his mouth and swallowed them with the rest of his beer. He was grateful the last of the pills would lessen this morning's throbbing head but was also disheartened in knowing the chase to find more would soon begin.

The truck's horn bellowed.

"ALL RIGHT! ALL RIGHT!" John grunted.

He threw on some sweatpants, a hoodie, and slipped on his permanently laced tennis shoes. He drove Maggie to school trying hard not to throw up while he waited anxiously for the alcohol and opiates to kick in and soothe him.

As they pulled into the high school parking lot, John reflected on how many times he'd performed this exhausting regimen of dropping Maggie off at school after a night of partying. Whether it was elementary, middle, or now high school, he loathed how often he'd pulled up feeling like complete dog shit. He observed all the fresh-faced kids bounding towards their classrooms. The teachers smiled and waved at parents and students. Everyone embraced a cheerful morning while

John delivered every ounce of energy he had just to complete this menial parental duty. He faked a smile, faked a wave at the crossing guard.

John even started teaching Maggie to drive years ago when she was twelve, anticipating that soon she could drive herself so he could nurse his brutal hangovers in bed without having to get up to take her. He cared little then that Maggie needed to be sixteen to legally drive. If she can die of Covid, he rationalized, then she can sure as shit drive a car before sixteen. So, for years John would sit in the passenger seat of the family truck barking out instructions while Maggie, with hands at 10 and 2, would peer over the steering wheel driving to the store or soccer practice. She was an excellent driver considering all the idiots on the road with valid licenses.

Today he needed the family's only car, though, so John had to drop his daughter off at high school like he'd done all those years prior. He needed it so he could restock and restore his addiction. They pulled into the drop-off area. John again feared Maggie would smell last night's residue of alcohol stench as they did their ritualistic kiss goodbye and said, "I love you."

He always left her with his daily words of wisdom. Maggie had heard it so much she stopped listening

years ago, but John repeated it regardless.
"If you hear something that sounds like firecrackers, you do not shelter in place. You run your ass off. Serpentine style. I'll pick you up at Shakey's."

Maggie had heard this direction since she was in elementary school. Her father educated her on how difficult it is to hit a moving target with a bullet, so he instructed her not to listen to teachers and cower in a classroom like a sitting duck.

"Take off running! You have my permission. I'll meet you at the pizza joint downtown, Shakey's."

By now John had hoped his orders were ingrained. In the world we live, it can happen anywhere. It's just how it is. It was so pathetic hearing politicians and pretty much anyone speaking to the public saying that repeated and rehearsed blather, "Our thoughts and prayers go out." They echo.

That sentiment was a completely insensitive thing to barf out, he'd think. The shootings were so commonplace that the authorities or officials that offered the canned condolences seemed as numb to the tragedies as the public was. They'd say it for a few days and move on with life. John felt that all those meaningless moments of silence should be switched to all out screams for change because silence, after all, changes nothing.

He said goodbye with an embrace and pretended Maggie didn't smell the disgusting residue. But she always did. Next, he drove down to McDonald's for more disgusting hangover calories. Two sausage breakfast sandwiches and a large OJ. Later John returned home. The relief from his drugs had finally settled in. He jumped back in bed, put his head between two pillows, and assumed his "leave me alone, world" hiding position. He slept off another morning until almost 1:00 p.m. at which point he had the strength to get up and start all over again.

But this afternoon, like many before it, John went to his trusty medicine container. He had hoped to shed the pain he felt.  Like many before it, today's pain was just as mental as it was physical. He understood this was why he continued down this destructive path. Staying sober and enduring the brutal discomfort that came with it was much too difficult. It was just easier to get high, so, day after day, he'd rinse and repeat his consumption. Today's anguish magnified, however, when he remembered that he was out of pills. Within minutes he was on the phone to his lifelong friend and fellow addict, JD.

"You a holder?" John asked, fingers and toes crossed.

"Of course, come over," JD replied.

"Oh, thank goodness."

John had known JD since high school. JD was, as they say, "wheels off crazy."  A hyper intelligent man who years earlier was a successful banker but had allowed addiction and alcoholism to derail his life completely. Where he was once married with two young kids and a white picket fence surrounding an expensive suburban home in a wealthy neighborhood in an affluent town, JD now rented a room from a deranged woman in her trashed house. They both drank themselves into oblivion each night. JD had two army cots in his tiny room, side by side, so when his young son came over, they slept on the cots below a small television set that constantly blared *Fox News*.

The owner of the home was a total train wreck. Her house was so cluttered there was only a tight path between unpacked boxes, laundry, and beat up furniture that led you around the home like a hiking trail. Each time John went to the house to buy the pills he was amazed at the endless amount of vodka bottles that lined the various tables and countertops along the trail. He couldn't judge though. When John would go on his benders his recycling bin was so full of empty beer bottles that when the recycle trucks came once a week the sound of all those bottles crashing into the truck's bed was so loud he wondered if the driver or neighbors thought his was a fraternity house rather than the home of a single man.

He arrived at JD's, engaged in some small talk with the trainwreck owner, who was of course hammered, and pretended he was interested in her blather. He then ran upstairs to JD's bedroom to repeat a transaction he'd done many times and spent thousands of dollars doing.

"How many oxy you got?" John asked.

"I've got 15 oxy and 25 yellow birds," said JD.

Yellow birds are the nickname JD branded these Norco opioid pills years ago when they had a yellow color. They had since gone white because the pharma companies produced so many millions of these pills they didn't have time to color them or perhaps the yellow coloring was an added expense. But JD liked the old name because it reminded him of a time they only needed one or two pills to enjoy an evening. Both men's tolerance and full-blown addiction had increased their intake substantially by now so those days were long gone. John loved JD.  He'd watched him basically lose everything over the years. JD's wife, kids, home, career were all a thing, or things, of the past. Although his young son would often come for a couple of days and they'd pretend they were in the military while they reclined on the cots and watched a war movie on the tiny television. But John looked past JD's decline. They were loyal lifelong friends. They were intelligent men with a great sense of humor and they continued to entertain each other through hilarious banter. And JD had the junk John wanted and they loved to get wasted which was another trait they obviously had in common.

"So how much you want this time?" JD asked.

"All of it," John replied. "Closed a great deal, got some funds."

John also knew JD was basically ripping him off with what he charged for the pills. But he didn't seem to mind. Not only was he desperate to feel better, but part of him felt he was supporting his friend financially. John, being a single dad, felt sorry for JD's son and deep down hoped he was helping JD pay for his son's needs. But mainly he needed the junk to feel better so at these moments he'd pay anything. So, with that, our hero swallowed a few yellow birds, raised up off the army cot, and instantly felt better.

The birds did their thing rather quickly and John navigated back through the cluttered maze of a hoarder's paradise out the door and into his car sporting a huge smile. Those pills are magical and can alleviate any hangover quickly. John was still dog tired, though, from last night's onslaught. He knew he was expected at the golf course but today, like so many others before it, there was no fucking way he was golfing. His pillow sandwich beckoned and he needed to get back to bed quickly.

He considered stopping at McDonald's again on the way home to power down another sausage McMuffin and OJ might help induce a food coma, but a quick glance down to the thick layer of blubber that surrounded his waist thankfully deterred him. Of course, John wanted to lose the tire and get in shape, but today he could barely crawl back into bed. Thank goodness he put out the garbage bins last night because he didn't have the strength or energy to do such an ordinary menial task right now.

The garbage truck pulled up just as John drove into his garage. He looked into the rearview mirror and admired the sanitation guys. They're there every week. Consistent. Hard working. Reliable. Everything John was not.  As another of his bins, overwhelmed by beer bottles, crashed into the sanitation truck, it sounded as if thunder was full of glass bottles. Again, John wondered if the neighbors thought he had a house party. He was totally embarrassed that only he had produced that many empties. The sound of the crashing bottles hitting the truck's metal walls could be compared to a crowded bowling alley that used glass pins. He slumped in his truck's seat trying to hide from embarrassment. John's home was a fraternity, all right. A fraternity of one.

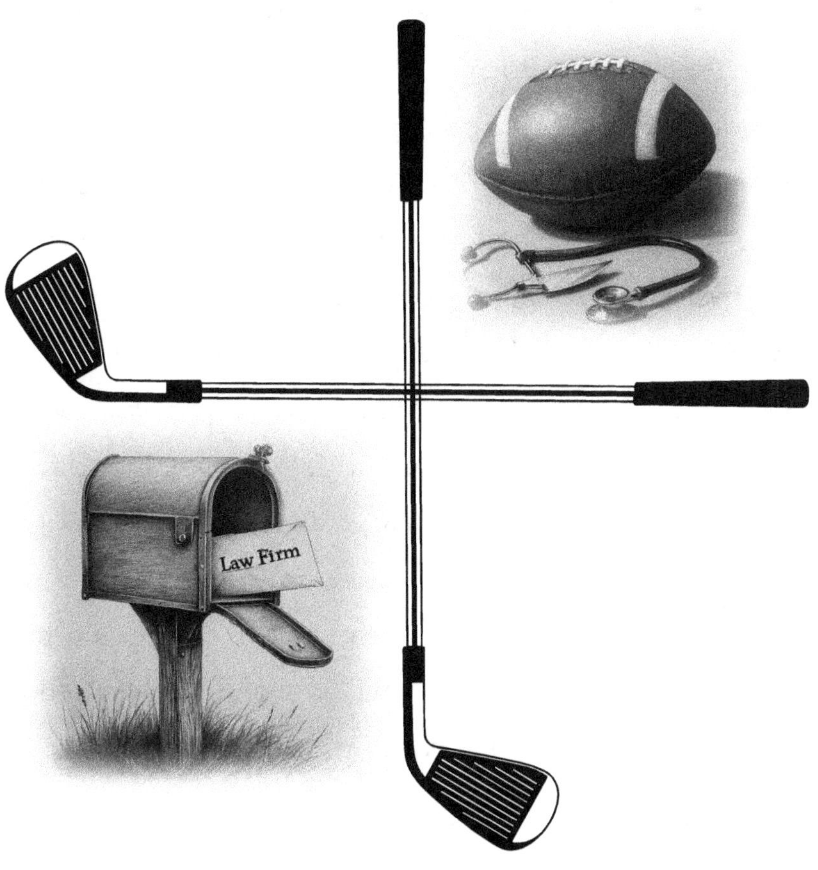

Law Firm

## HOLE #2

There's a photograph of John Harrison hanging in his garage. It's of him in a college football uniform coming off the field. His uniform is noticeably clean. John was a very good player, but he had already suffered major injuries in high school that required extensive surgeries by the time he'd reached college.  But he had ambitions as a young kid. He grew up watching his college team play and, being the dreamer he was, was determined to play for the University of California. He'd wear a knee brace and shoulder harness and felt he was literally surviving as opposed to playing. He did achieve his goal. But more injuries cut his playing days short.

Before a practice as he sat on the trainer's table getting his ankles taped this wiley old trainer looked at young John with all his scars lining his body and in his long Texas draw said, "Son, why do you continue to play this game?"

John had no logical answer. Was it his belligerent father that barely spoke to him, constantly telling him he'd never amount to shit? Was he determined to prove his father wrong even though that meant permanently damaging himself?  He always felt it a bit absurd that as the years went on he was portrayed as the guy that played football at Cal when he knew inside that he'd had a cup of coffee at best and that's exactly what he told anyone that asked him about his playing days.

However, time has a funny way of manipulating mediocrity so with his old football prowess, the older he got, the better he was. John was now a fully middle-aged man with a prototypical beer belly to prove it. He had tried many ventures in life, from sportscasting to rock musician to actor. He was the lead singer in a band that never made any money other than beer money at the venues they played. He landed a few TV commercials and had somehow talked his way into a speaking role on a prime time NBC cop show shot in San Francisco that was canceled after one season because *Dancing with the Stars* crushed it in the ratings. He had to join the actors' union to do the part which cost him $1,300. The role paid $1,000, so the irony was he'd actually "paid" to make his debut as a tough cop that got into a bar fight.  He was fine with it. After all, this speaking role was a huge step up from the time he played an assassin, dressed in a chef's outfit, while holding a gun, experience a life flashing before your eyes moment when Chuck Norris performed a roundhouse kick that came barely an inch from his nose during an episode of *Walker Texas Ranger.*

John simply liked to try things. He considered himself an expert at everything, champion of nothing. But as his attempts at doing anything but normal work disintegrated and he got wiser, he took a job as an insurance salesman and moved back to California. He found a beautiful woman to marry and grew that belly, along with a family. People always say the day their first child is born absolutely changes things. John, being the anti-establishment man he'd always been, didn't buy it. What he did feel, however, was that Maggie gave him purpose. He never slept well when Maggie was a baby always getting out of bed to check her crib making sure she was breathing. He knew if he couldn't be one of the many things he tried in life, he was determined to be a good father. Of course, that definition could fluctuate based on his behavior at times but he loved Maggie as much as anyone can love their child. And even though he had some, what others would deem unacceptable, habits, loving and caring for Maggie wasn't an issue. You see, John felt he was trying and doing the very best he could.

Unfortunately, the woman he married thought he was a complete fucking loser and never hesitated to beat him down mentally and emotionally. Locked front doors leading to hotel overnights became so common in their early years of marriage that it was almost a relief to divorce. He needed to get Maggie away from the toxicity.  Even if it was for only 50% of her life. The night he spent Christmas Eve in the county lockup because, after taking a knee to his balls and scratches to his face, the police looked at his gorgeous wife and, while one cop handed her his personal phone number if she ever "needed anything" and the other one cuffed him, they of course deemed him the aggressor.  John decided this wasn't a final straw but rather a fracking rig that sucked every bit of gas out of the relationship. The divorce was simple.

Although he hated sharing Maggie. She was only three at the time but he was determined that even though he'd only get Maggie 50% of the time, she was going to get 100% of his attention.  Maggie's mom tried a handful of times over the next few years to get full custody by dragging John to court. It got so that he would duck while gently opening his mailbox and peek into it with one eye open as if the Unabomber had sent him a package while praying her lawyer hadn't sent another one of his thick envelopes summoning him to court again. One custody battle even cost him $35K defending himself from some ludicrous accusations.

But after six ridiculous months in court it was determined, after an interview with four-year-old Maggie, that the worst thing her father had done, in her own words, was "He makes me eat carrots."

You see, John had some habits, some may even say faults. He was human. But nobody was going to take away his God-given right to be a father to the one thing that mattered most.

26

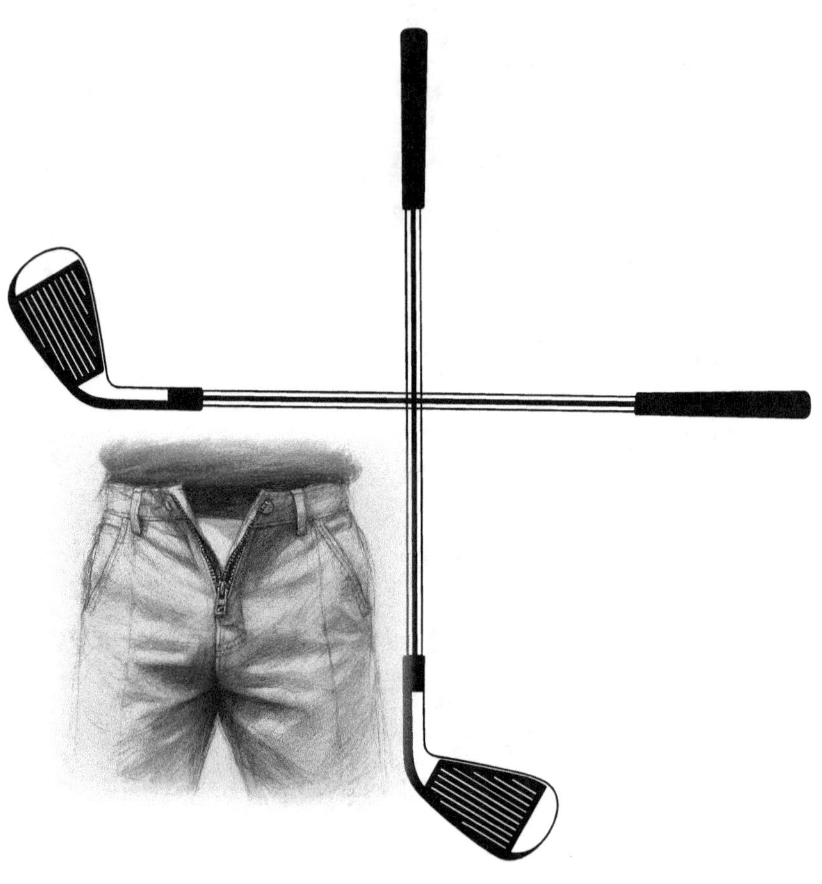

## HOLE #3

What's in a nickname?

"I can't hold it; I'm going to burst!" said John Harrison.

"I'm not surprised, you've drunk enough beer to drown a horse," his playing partner scoffed, creating a laugh amongst the group.

"You guys go, I gotta take a leak," instructed John.

Even though he had made birdie on 17, which, according to accepted golf protocol, gave him honors to hit first on the next tee, there was no way he could hold it any longer. His playing partners understood. Though none of them wanted to "step" on a birdie" as they say and hit before him, this was one of those moments where they all obliged.

"Here come the ladies, you better push hard," Chris yelled toward John.

The 18th tee box at Eagle Vista Country Club was a mere 30 yards from the green on the first hole. Like clockwork, every Saturday the men would be on the 18th tee box finishing their round while the first foursome of the women's group putted on the first green, just starting theirs. Only a large pine separated the distance from 1 green to 18 tee, but the tree's trunk was wide enough to block the view. That is, if you did your business quickly.

"You better hurry, dude. Here they come," one of the men barked at John, who was in full stream against the pine's trunk, hidden from the women.

"I'm trying.  Shit, I can't stop it now!" John yelled to his group who were enjoying his plight.

Suzanne finished her putt and all four women jumped in their carts to drive past the 18th tee on their way to the 2nd hole. John loved Suzanne, always had. She was a knockout and he'd always tried to show her the man he could be, not the man he was. If she caught him relieving his beer bursting bladder against the trunk of this pine, all the work he'd put in wooing Suzanne and showing her how classy he was would be destroyed. He pushed as hard as he could as the women got closer and closer.

John was moments away from being outed in more ways than one when he made the terrible decision to hastily push his manhood back into his pants and simultaneously yank hard on his zipper so the rapidly approaching Suzanne would not see him peeing on the tree.

"OHHHHH SHIIIIITT!" was the scream that bellowed from the base of the tall pine. In his haste, John had not properly restored his manhood into a safe position and his zipper caught its soft tissue right at the top. The zipper's teeth tore into the sensitive skin producing a blood curdling scream that only a man with a similar experience of catching his unit in his zipper could relate to. John hastily bent forward and violently tugged down on his zipper to release the teeth but it was too late. His scream had drawn the attention not only of his buddies, who all winced in pain at the visual of what John had just done, but also the four women driving by. All of them wore a look of complete disgust by what they had just witnessed.

Men peeing on trees was nothing new, but it was frowned upon at Eagle Vista. Mostly by the ladies. Good nicknames happen spontaneously. And when it's a good one it sticks on someone forever. From that moment on John Harrison's real name was forever lost in the roar of laughter that followed and subsequent express train of speed in which this event spread throughout the entire club. From this point on John Harrison would never be called by his birth name again. Going forward, to every friend, fellow member, and employee at Eagle

Vista Country Club, he was appropriately and simply called "Zip."

## HOLE #4

*THWAAK!* It's 8:00 a.m. at Eagle Vista Country Club. A routine Saturday and another wayward tee shot headed for the townhomes that lined the right side of the fairway on this first hole. The player LH promptly reached into his pocket for another ball and another attempt.

"Breakfast ball," he announced to the group, notifying them that he was already cheating and that the first hack wouldn't be counted. But since most of the group called the club's bar their driving range, instead of warming up at the actual driving range, this breakfast ball was an accepted ritual. Why warm up when vodka and OJ work better?

"Anyone hear from Zip?" someone in the group asked, as they muddled around the first tee box ready to start their day.

"No, he's going to bail again. Fuck him."

"But he's our fourth! Fuck it, we'll go without him, again. So tired of this shit."

It was simply a gorgeous morning at Eagle Vista. Why it's called Eagle Vista is a mystery as an actual eagle has never been within hundreds of miles of this place. Crows, however, are abundant. Any breakfast sandwich or hot dog left in a golf cart unattended while a golfer is a mere 10 feet away holding an object that can easily be helicoptered at one of those obnoxious ravens does not deter the crows from snatching said breakfast sando or $10 hot dog from the cart and soaring off into the blue.  Some have suggested carrying pellet guns in golf bags. Not to actually kill the flying rats. But simply to "message" them that their thievery won't be tolerated.

Then there are the snow geese that decades ago used to come only in warm winter months but have now decided the area is a year-round habitat. These land sharks are a serious pain in the ass. Constantly eating and gouging the manicured fairways while their constant pecking produces constant shitting. Avoiding stepping in the small land mines has become an art form. And these mines aren't small! These geese are huge and can leave shit the size that can rival any golden retriever, but, unfortunately, without the owner there to pick it up. Often a line drive shot off a club would drill one of these feeding geese. No sorrow was felt by the golfer who just plugged the goose. In fact, accolades were given and "kill that chicken!" had been yelled a time or two.

To counter the geese infestation, the general manager of Eagle Vista hired a local widow to run her Border Collie sheep dog at the geese in hopes they'd take flight and find a local park to have their shitting parties. The collie was useless, however. The pea-brained geese had figured out they could take flight from the oncoming full sprint collie right at the last minute and then fly a few hundred yards to another fairway only to start dotting that part of the course with their digestive gifts. Essentially the collie just helped in spreading the geese shit proportionately around the entire course. The dog simply was getting exercise while no one had the heart to inform the owner that her dog was worthless because she was a recent widow and had everyone's sympathy.

"I sent Zip a text. No response. Standard. Fuck him, we go without him . . . again," LH grumbled.

*THWAAK!* LH hammered another grounder off the first tee. Eagle Vista is a mighty 6,000-yard track which each member is damn proud of, yet loves to criticize. Eagle Vista is one of the more affordable private clubs in this affluent, little suburban town full of baseball cap wearing soccer moms driving SUVs on their way to Pilates. The town was once just orchards. Peaches, almonds, apples, as far as one could see.

There was one railroad track through a two-street town nestled below sweeping hills separating the town from the San Francisco Bay area by about 30 miles. But developers saw a commuters' gold mine in this once lazy two-street town with the single agricultural railroad and started to bulldoze those orchards. And with that came the development of Eagle Vista Country Club.

The track homes around the golf course were a bit smaller and more affordable than surrounding developments and, thus, attracted a more blue-collar type of buyer. Subsequently, Eagle Vista CC attracted a similar member. Not obnoxiously wealthy. But a hard worker that loved the game of golf and was proud to have earned enough to afford this less affluent, less swanky, less pretentious club. Of course, other clubs in the area were more expensive and affluent. But that's what made Eagle Vista shine. You just can't swing your dick at Eagle Vista like they do at the other places. But you can still criticize. And, oh, do they. It's part of paying dues.

It's a human characteristic to want to be critical when, since they pay for it, folks feel entitled to criticize the place and how it has been maintained and managed. It is actually just a bad habit. After all, bitching and negativity can be more interesting than being positive. It is similar to gossip which isn't positive at all but, oh, isn't it interesting. Eagle Vista has its own particular character, meaning you're not going to get Augusta conditions at Joe Beer Belly Muni prices. But it is a tough track.

Many guests have come to Eagle Vista, looked at its 6,000 yards, and labeled it a pitch and putt.  It's been called Fenway. Short porch. Or My Little Pony CC. But dollars to donuts every time a golfer discounted Eagle Vista they got humbled. It is short but NARROW. Those small affordable homes that lined the fairways seemed to cartoonishly expand, narrowing said fairways even more after a few wayward shots found their backyards. Players that discounted Eagle Vista would soon start to realize if you spray, you pay.

Zip's iPhone blasted out the sound of an old car horn: "AROOOGHA! AROOOGHA!"

It was so fucking loud and annoying, but Zip used that particular sound simply because it was the only sound obnoxious enough to roust him from his slumber. He reached for his phone to check the text he received. It was from LH, who damn well knew by this point that Zip ain't making the tee time. But LH was so vexatious he texted anyway. He couldn't help it. His Rain Man brain was simply wired that way.

*You making it?* LH asked.

Zip groaned as he read. Then sent a reply: *Sorry, my daughter had some trouble at school so I have to deal with it. You guys go on without me.*

Two things. The group already started playing without Zip because they were obviously accustomed to his no-shows. Secondly, just as he pressed send, he wondered had he used this same "daughter in trouble" excuse recently? Zip had several go-to excuses on cue when he needed them and daughter in trouble was a solid one because it returned no recourse. Obviously, no one could get upset with him with that one. He also became accustomed to using: *I don't feel well,* which was never questioned anymore due to Covid.

Since Zip sold life insurance for a living, which absolutely enabled his lifestyle because he was self-employed and never had a boss question where he was in the morning, he often told the group one of his clients died and he needed to deal with the claim. Lastly, if he had used the others too frequently, he could always say his mom had a health scare, or father, sister, or brother, he used so many times you'd think he had a sprawling family. Which he didn't.

But there was no response from LH which wasn't a surprise because nobody honestly cared. LH simply sent the text due to his neurosis. But the car horn and text exchange were enough to frazzle Zip awake. And though the pills he swallowed with his McDonald's OJ made him feel better and induced another three to four hours of sleep, it was now 1:00 p.m. and his guilt and self-loathing had resurfaced. Enough so that he dragged his ass out of bed, looked into his mirrored closet doors at the middle-aged loser he'd become, and stumbled down the hall to the kitchen. For guess what? Yes, another beer. He loved Red Stripe and was grateful he hadn't finished off last night's 12 pack. Or was it an18 pack? Who cared? There were a few left, thank God. So, after a few mighty gulps that included two to three pills he'd bought from JD that morning, in no time he felt that warm wrapper of booze and pills.

What would he do today? Spend some time callously swiping human beings on some dating apps? Perhaps there'd be a few text exchanges with some women knowing full well he felt way too much self-loathing and inner disgust to ever actually date. Maybe he'd do it just to feel relevant. Like so many on those apps, he craved to know if he was still attractive to someone. Zip yearned for human contact. He wanted to pretend he was attractive enough to possibly date someone but deep down he knew he wasn't. His act was the opposite of clean.

This swiping dance was a complete waste of time. These were actual people being swiped away which was such a demeaning action. But that's how it was. He already knew he'd never see any of these women. Most were so random with their commonality.  It seemed as if every one of them said that they liked wine and hiking. You'd have thought the hills around the area would be full of drunk women! Why does every woman say they want a man that can make them laugh? Damn that's a lot of pressure! He wondered if a woman would find it funny that he was a middle-aged, unattractive, beer-bellied drug addict? He thought not.

So, after a few "Hey, I loved your profile" or "Do you like comedy shows?" Zip was determined today would not be a rinse and repeat day of him sitting at his kitchen table scouring the internet while slamming another 14 Red Stripes and handfuls of yellow birds. Something he loved to do. He could spend hours on TMZ's site seeing how celebs supposedly lived. Did he envy the countless pictures of celebrities on the decks of yachts in the Mediterranean always ostensibly living it up? Did these people ever have problems? And how about Bezos in his tailored T-shirts that hugged his jacked arms while he lounged on his bazillion-dollar yacht? Those arms were an obvious result of human growth hormone, testosterone injections, and Ozempic cocktails as opposed to him spending countless hours doing dumbbell curls in the gym. But, hey, how else can a Mr. Clean-looking gremlin compensate for the nerd years he endured as a youth?

"When's the cage match with Zuckerberg?" Zip chuckled to himself. After his pill and booze glow kicked in, Zip often wisecracked and laughed to himself, of course, because there was no one around to listen. And what's with these billionaire nerds getting so jacked and training MMA as they age? Zip scoured TMZ for some celeb DUI mugshots. Those were great. But he loved Mondays during football season so he could watch videos of idiot NFL fans wearing their $150 team jerseys living in complete fantasyland pretending they were actually a part of said team just beating the living shit out of each other in the stands, bathrooms, and stadium conclaves. Why did they always try to fight one-handed while holding that $20 beer in the other hand? Because it was a fucking $20 beer, that's why! Zip loved when they'd fight and drop their beer to the ground. It always created an instant ice rink and without fail would send these out of shape, brawling patrons slipping and slamming to the ground.

"Down goes Frazier."

The jersey would be yanked upward exposing a massive beer belly. The irony was these fat-ass, stumbling, drunk brawlers never wore a lineman's number on their jersey, which they appropriately should have. The videos always showed 100 lb. overweight fat fucks wearing a wide receiver or quarterback number which did a complete disservice to the actual ripped athletic player whose number the jersey replicated. And if it was a special Monday, sometimes TMZ had a couple women just throwing down. These broads would flat out bring it. They never quit. Just a hair ripping, face scratching, all out melee.

But today was not a day for TMZ.  Zip was determined to do something today. After all, his buzz was perfect and the sun was shining, so he hopped in his chipped paint, one flat tire, beat to shit golf cart a neighbor had given him and decided to head to the driving range to hit some golf balls. His golf cart was an eyesore, but he cared less. The price was right. Since he only owned one vehicle, most days Maggie took it to school leaving Zip with his "EV" as he called it. They lived inside a gated community that contained rows of small stucco homes surrounding Eagle Vista CC and since Zip worked from home and his life, if you can call it one, centered around Eagle Vista, he barely left the neighborhood. Except those days he finished his beer supply on the previous night's bender.

Without hesitation Zip would hop in the golf cart that could reach speeds of 25 miles per hour and head out the gate down the sidewalks to his local grocery store for rinse and repeat supplies. He cared less about the looks he'd get from drivers on the road wondering why a man in a golf cart would be cruising in the opposite direction of traffic down a sidewalk. Maggie had the car, so what was he to do? He needed beer. Never mind that he'd heard rumors that the cackling hens on the local Next Door website would write about the lawbreaking man, sporting a hoodie and sunglasses, driving down the sidewalk!

*Get a life*, he thought. Besides he'd only seen a cop once or twice and those guys cared little to stop and question him.

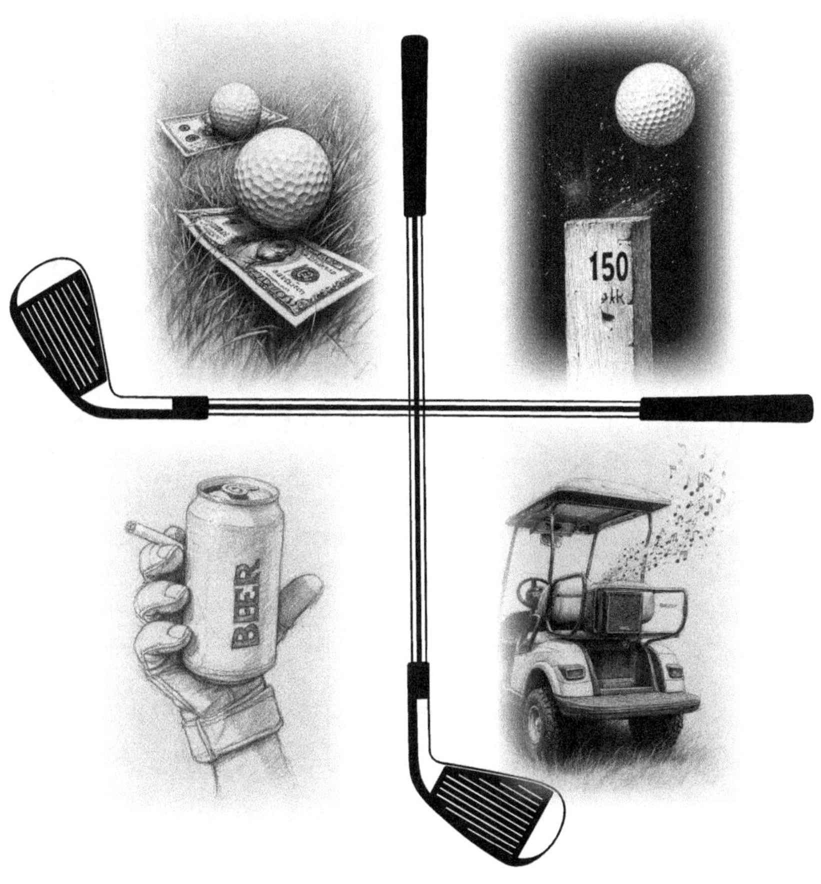

150

BEER

## HOLE #5

Now the driving range at Eagle Vista was in no way respectable or nice. It wasn't close to the clubhouse as most ranges are either. It was a few minutes' drive from the actual course. Tucked away in a secluded patch of land that was once a cow pasture. In fact, on any given day 20 to 30 cows would sit a few feet away from the hitting mats separated only by a wire fence. It's not necessarily a nice facility and often has the waft of cow manure. But on a sunny day the light breezes swept across the tall grass in the hills that surrounded the dirt landscape where folks smacked golf ball after golf ball.

The EV range was beat up. However, it was peaceful, and it was ours, and could often remedy a shitty day. Or in Zip's case today, add a little joy to his buzz.

"Oh fuck, it's Carl the Complainer." Zip gulped as he pulled up to the range.

Carl was a long-time member. A grizzly, old retired banker that once played some college golf and had actually won the San Francisco City Championship sometime in the early '60s. Nobody gave a shit but Carl, so if you asked him about it just to fuck with him, he'd tell you a teenage Johnny Miller played in it too, which was Carl's claim to fame. The complainer moniker was earned because Carl is just one of those guys that never had a good thing to say about anything associated with Eagle Vista. Every club has one. And as mentioned earlier, he figured his monthly dues gave him a ticket to just bitch. And bitch he did. About everything.

Zip pulled up and greeted Carl and just as Carl pried his lips open Zip announced, "Hey, Carl, it's a no whining Wednesday. No complaining today. It's beautiful out and we're keeping it positive. What's shakin'?"

"Oh fuck, something's wrong with the picker so I had to collect my own balls," Carl griped, ignoring Zip's request.

This wasn't such a bad thing, Zip thought, because Carl was all of 5'5" pushing 200 lbs. so any physical activity he did was a good thing. Just then a ball smacked off the 100-yard metal post sounding like a bowler picking up a corner pin!

"This fucking guy," Carl grumbled, motioning to a slender player hitting balls on a bluff above the range that is cordoned off for private lessons.

"What's his deal?" Zip asked

"Oh, he's some new member. Thinks he's hot shit . . . cocksucker shouldn't be up there in the private area," Carl griped. "Word is he had a cup of coffee on Korn Ferry."

"What's he doing at this dog track then?" Zip asked, noticing the guy's fluid swing.

"Who knows, but he's been here a week and he's already disrespecting the dress code too," Carl fumed.

Now Eagle Vista was no swanky joint but the wife beater and jeans the guy was wearing was pushing it, not to mention him blasting Guns and Roses from his golf cart speakers while exhaling cigarette smoke downhill into everyone's noses.

"I've heard he played here once and was five under. I've talked to him but he blew me off like I didn't exist, cocksucker," Carl continued.

*BANG!* Another ball hit the 150-yard pole.

"Fucking show off!" Carl yelled. "Hey, if you're so fucking good what are you doing here? And you're not supposed to be in that area!"

And just then, true to form, Carl pulled out his cell phone and called the pro shop. "Hey, this is Carl."

You could almost hear the kid in the pro shop who answered Carl's complaint roll his eyes and murmur, "Here we go."

"This new guy, I guess his last name is Biggs, is hitting balls from the restricted teaching area and he's got his golf cart up there killing the grass and blasting his music. It's fucking annoying!" Carl barked into his phone.

"Okay, we'll get someone up there," the kid replied, as he hung up with absolutely no intention of sending anyone to the range to talk to Biggs.

Zip wasn't so irritated at first. After all he'd never seen a pro, Korn Ferry or not, at the illustrious Eagle Vista CC. Zip liked that a talented player joined there. He'd rather have really good players there than the normal octogenarians hitting 30-yard grounders, also known as Havercamps, while plodding around in five-hour-plus rounds like it was nothing. He sat back and watched Biggs just pound the yardage poles actually hitting the metal every third or fourth shot and marveled at Bigg's buttery swing all while a cigarette hung from his mouth.

So, Zip, being a take no shit instigator, decided to join Carl with some ribbing of Biggs. As Biggs lit another nail Zip yelled, "Hey, thanks for letting us enjoy your cigarettes too!"

Biggs didn't acknowledge either of them. Just kept banging posts.

"Told you he was an asshole," Carl said.

Just then a ball screamed past Carl and Zip. A head high line drive just in front of them that didn't stop until it nailed the ball machine inside the small wooden range shack. It left a nice dent in the machine. Carl glared at Biggs, who laughed earnestly at both Carl and Zip's reaction to seeing a laser beam of a ball flash in front of them. Merely a foot away from decapitating them.

"That's it, motherfucker. I'm calling the cops!" Carl screamed, as he hastily reached into his back pocket for his cell phone.

"No, no, Carl, don't do that. He's just fucking around," Zip said. He had a mind to go wrap his 9 iron around Biggs' head but Biggs' laughter somewhat touched Zip's rebel side and he was actually impressed by Biggs' accuracy.

By then Carl had had enough. "I'm going to the shop. This guy's an asshole and they're going to hear about it!" He briskly walked to his cart and beelined it to the club to gripe to any and all. In fact, a few hours later when Zip was at the club's bar known as the Eagles Nest, or just The Nest for the many EV regulars, Zip was approached no less than five times from patrons asking what went down at the range. When

Carl had new material to complain about, he was like a friggin' gripe tornado whipping through the club sharing with anyone that unfortunately hadn't seen him coming.

"Hey, nice shot. I'm Zip." He introduced himself to Biggs and extended his closed hand to fist bump.

"Hey, I'm Biggs."

"Good to meet you, you new?" Zip asked.

"Yeah, I joined last week. Nice track for a pitch and putt," Biggs replied, with a cocky smile. His cigarette dangled precariously on the end of his bottom lip.

Zip immediately wished the tight confines that Eagle Vista presented with the looming townhomes that lined the fairways could make Biggs eat those words, but Carl had already told him that Biggs shot five under. Or perhaps it could be more of the same bullshit that spewed around Eagle Vista. Carl was a leader in the bullshit department.

"Look, I know we're outside but that cigarette is fucking carrying across the range. Makes the cow's methane seem tolerable," Zip told Biggs.

Biggs pulled the cigarette from his mouth and extinguished it on the beautiful grass with a stomp from his tattered tennis shoes. "You know that old dude?" Biggs asked, referring to Carl.

"Yeah, he's a bit of an acquired taste," Zip replied

"He's a fucking range Nazi. I've been here a week and he's called the pro shop three times, ratting me out about shit!"

"Just try to ignore him. But if you make his complaint list . . . beware." Zip laughed, now warming to anyone that saw Carl for the tool that he was.

"That message pitch I sent at you guys wasn't for you, trust me," Biggs told Zip, as he reached into his bag for a different club to hit.

"So, what's your deal, you're a pro?" Zip queried.

"Yeah, I gave it a run. Played professionally a handful of years. Never got my tour card though. Was really close. Took a triple on the last hole of a qualifier in South Carolina that cost me big time."

"No shit? What happened?" Zip enthusiastically asked, as he'd never met anyone with that kind of game.

"Oh, it was the finishing hole with water down the left side. My go-to shot off the tee when I need to hit a fairway finder is a high cut and this hole was perfectly set for that. Right in my backswing some asshole yelled, 'You suck!' and I totally shanked my shot. Hit a low hook straight into the water crossing in only about 50 yards from the tee. I was so pissed I duck hooked my next shot into the lake again. Took a 7. No tour card," Biggs explained, seemingly without bitterness.

"Well, that totally blows. Did you confront the dude or at least glare at him?" Zip pressed, trying for more info.

"No, he took off. Heard he had a $20 bet on the guy I was playing. I'm telling you these gambling sites with their in-round betting lines. It's a matter of time before someone screams out while a player's putting to win The Masters or the US Open. I mean who cares, right? The guy will get kicked out but he'll win his piddly $20 bet!"

"You ever play against any big names?" Zip continued pressing, as he casually swung a wedge through the grass.

"Yeah, I mean I didn't play with anyone big during my time on Korn Ferry. Mainly because I wasn't around long enough. But I was in a junior tourney with Bryson. That was before his juicing years." Biggs chuckled.

"Seriously? You think he juiced?"

"I mean compare photos of his earlier years to the Hulk years. I obviously don't have evidence, but 50 pounds of muscle is a whole lot of banana smoothies he claimed to drink. Wasn't it obvious? And the tour loved the attention so their so-called testing was a sham. The tour raked in millions because people were tuning in to see if he could hit one 400 yards. Look at the photos of guys like McGuire, A-Rod, or Bonds before they juiced. Bryson was the same. I mean McGuire looked like a fucking lumberjack and he couldn't even button his jersey to the top. Tiger did the same. Sure, he hit the gym but he was a skinny dork and then he's some jacked dude! Very top-heavy too, like McGuire and Bryson. It's no wonder they had foot and leg issues. You can't add that kind of weight to your upper body and not have it wear down on your skinny sticks holding you up. Tiger's the type to juice too. Insecure dweeb of a teen finds super stardom and doesn't know how to handle it.  Completely dominated by his folks. He was just a dweeb and couldn't handle the limelight. And, yes, he is solely responsible for making golf cool and bringing the athletes to golf away from football, hoops, and baseball. But a nerd is a nerd is a nerd. Not sure dudes like Jordan or Barkley, with all their vices, were the best role models if you know what I mean. But, yeah, I met him on a putting green once. Before a tourney in San Francisco. I told him he inspired me to pick up golf. Told him my name was Thomas Biggs and right away he started calling me one of these stupid fucking nicknames he gives everyone. It was "Bigsy" or some shit. Totally stupid but made him feel superior. He's a tool."

Zip was all ears at this point. Totally relishing on the rant his new acquaintance, Thomas Biggs, was offering. "That's hilarious. I think he's a d-bag too!" Zip chimed in enthusiastically. "Although all my bros give each other nicknames too."

"No, don't get me wrong. It's just the way he goes about it. Like he's tryin to be cool because he was such a dork as a kid. Seems forced," Biggs continued.

"How 'bout all the cheating? I mean my ex was a smoke show and we fought like cats and dogs. I couldn't understand how such a beautiful exterior could surround such a cold, mean as a snake, person. I lost a lot of respect for Tiger cuz I had some chances to cheat on my wife but, as much as I couldn't stand her, I never did. Especially when she was pregnant! And with some Waffle House waitress!? Yeah, maybe you slip up and cheat once, but you don't have one broad after the other lined up like the Rockettes while your wife is home pregnant. And that press conference with his mom sitting there? Completely cringe-worthy TV. Whose idea was that?"

"Right! I know it was supposed to be a serious moment but I couldn't stop laughing," Biggs blurted out. "I mean the dude didn't cure cancer. He can hit a little white ball better than anyone else. So he fucked up. But since corporate America and the PGA invested millions in him, they gotta run him out there to fall on the sword to try to cover their asses. All the women got hosed. You're one of the only dudes I've met that thinks about him like I do."

"Yeah, you're right," Zip interjected. "Tiger did dominate and made golf seem cool. He didn't have the competition that today's game has though. More athletes are golfing now. It's a lot harder to go against Rory, DJ, Finau, Homa. Shit, Woodland played college hoops. Scotty's a BEAST and Burns and Wyndham are athletic as hell. I mean, Tiger would pull into the parking lot and see powder puffs like David Toms, Lee Jansen, Corey Pavin. Ernie was solid but Phil, with his collar turned up full pansy style, was already mentally beat before the first shot! Anyway, anyone else?" Zip asked.

"Not really. I talked to Koepka once. Riveting convo. It'd be more stimulating talking to a golf ball," Biggs snickered. "I did see Rahm split his pants once at the driving range. I wasn't in the tourney. Was just watching guys hit. This was before the Saudi money that allowed him to afford a tailor. Those off the rack pants he used to pour into that squeezed his fat ass just split right down the seams. He needs to mix in a salad every now and then instead of all the tomahawk steaks."

"So what happened? How come you're playing at this dump instead of playing for real money? You were on Korn Ferry?"

Biggs took a big gulp of his Budweiser. In fact, a double gulp, until it was gone. He tossed the can in the back basket of his golf cart making a clanging sound as if it ricocheted amongst the six or seven fellow empties. "Wounded," as he called them. He let out a huge BURP. Pulled out a vape pen and sucked a huge draw followed by an exhale cloud so huge his head disappeared for a second.

"Want a hit? It's sativa," Biggs asked, as he held back a choking cough.

"Absolutely!" Zip joyfully retorted, now starting to like Biggs even more.

The two of them immediately hit it off. Zip heard Led Zeppelin's "Kashmir" come on Bigg's phone that was connected to his Bluetooth speaker and immediately demanded, "Crank it up!"

To which Biggs obliged.

"Hey, let's try something," Zip asked. "I'll hand you a club and tell you which pole to go for. If you get within a 10-foot radius I'll give you a dollar. If you don't, you pay me. If it's really close then it's $2 and if you hit the post then that's $5. But if you totally shank one, or don't come within 20 yards, you owe me $5."

Biggs took another huge cloud-producing drag off his vape pen.

 "No problem, amigo."

"Here's the 60 degree. Hit the 100-yard post," Zip enthusiastically requested.

Biggs immediately banged a ball right off the side of the post with his first shot. Even the grazing cows' heads perked up.

"Goddamn!" Zip exclaimed, fully surprised.

"This is going to get expensive," Biggs wryly announced.

"9 iron, 150-yard pole?" Zip asked with purpose.

Biggs then effortlessly hit a buttery draw that landed within 10 feet. Zip next handed Biggs a 7 iron and said 175 and Biggs almost struck that post as well, barely missing.

"What are we at eight bucks?" Biggs asked.

"Yeah, shit. Do you take Venmo?" Zip replied. He needed to make the game harder, so he pulled out a 5 iron.

"Okay, tough guy, 200-yard pole."

"Draw or fade?" Biggs arrogantly asked.

"Take it easy, Arnie. Just try to get close."

Biggs promptly hit a high fade that came down, from what they could tell, within a 10-foot radius, but Zip was high and didn't want to lose so he argued that it was outside 10 feet. Zip could definitely see that Biggs had a skill level far past anything he'd ever witnessed. "Kashmir" was blasting. Biggs was plastering the yardage poles on demand. The cows even seemed impressed. Zip had found a new friend.

Just then the music abruptly stopped and a phone call interrupted the good vibes. Biggs turned to look at the phone on the seat of his cart. The phone ID said spam in bold letters, which Zip also noticed.

"Fucking spam. You get those too?" Zip asked. "I'm such a loser, only two people ever call me, my daughter and spam."

He then pulled out a wedge. He was now completely concerned that he was about to be down at least $10 in only a few minutes. Except there was no music blaring. The phone call had interrupted it. Only the peaceful sounds of nature could be heard. Even the nearby neighbor had taken a break from clearing leaves off his lawn with his obnoxious, blaring leaf blower sarcastically known as the California State Bird.  In these parts, in every neighborhood, every day, that shrilling leaf blower is all that's heard! In fact, there was no sound at all. No music, no leaf blower, no mooing cows. It was almost awkward.

Zip handed Biggs a wedge and said, "125 pole."

Biggs proceeded to shank his shot nowhere near the post, landing some 30 yards to the left.

"What the entire fuck?" Zip laughed. They actually both laughed. The miss was so bad it was bizarre.

Zip handed Biggs the same 60° wedge that Biggs had just used to smack a pole a minute ago and said, "This might cost me $5 bucks, but 100-yard pole." Once again Biggs' wedge came nowhere near the target. It wasn't a total shank like the last ball, but well outside the wagering parameters.

"Dude you're going to owe ME money!" Zip exclaimed, completely surprised by the sudden inaccuracy of Biggs' game. "What's going on?"

"I don't know. I think the weed fucked me up. I can't concentrate," Biggs admitted.

"No worries. We'll call it even," Zip countered. "I know you're new but have you found anyone to play with? I mean you'll kick the crap out of the guys I play with but it looks like you like to drink, so we can hang with you in that category."

"Sure, that sounds great," Biggs replied, somewhat excited that he had found a possible group to play with.

They exchanged phone numbers and farewells and Zip hopped in his beat-up golf cart. As he drove away, he noticed Biggs going back to his practice. He turned his music back on and started hitting crispy iron shots at the targets. Seemingly back to normal.

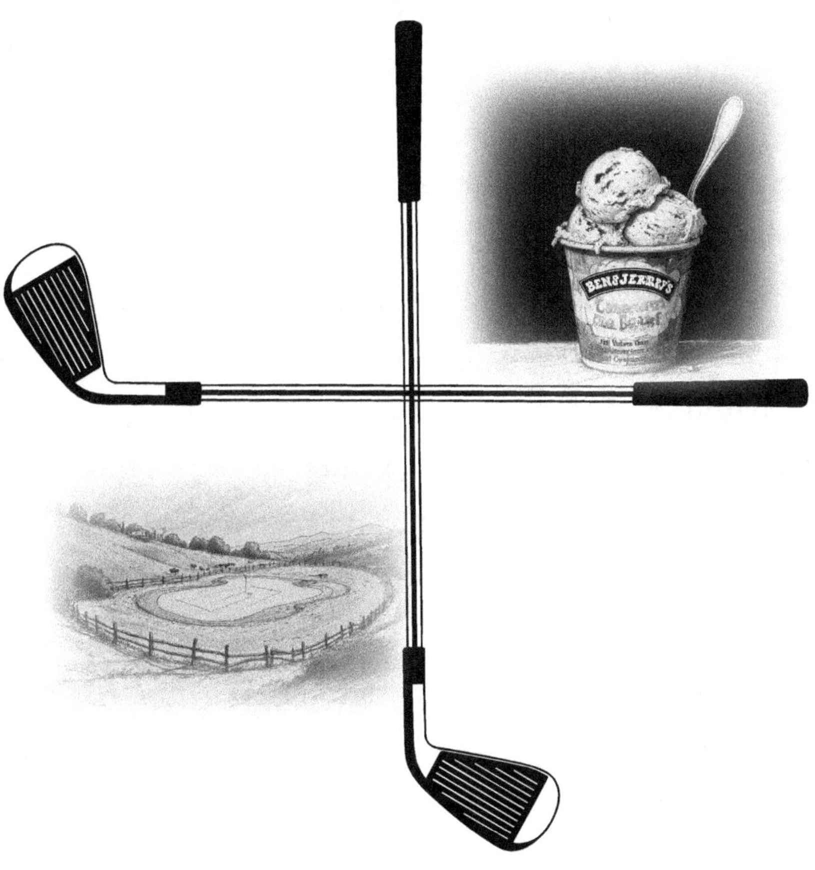

## HOLE #6

As Zip drove towards his house, he saw Maggie's boyfriend's truck parked in front. Jake, as he's named, must have given Maggie a ride home. Jake didn't impress Zip whatsoever. Not only did he have the same overused name that ostensibly one out of every three boys in this area share, but he was a total mama's boy in Zip's eyes. The word was Jake is some soccer star with ambitions that he is good enough to play in college. Zip had a football background. Played at a major college. Has the shoulder and knee scars to prove it. He knew what it took to play beyond high school, and although he was okay with Jake being a soccer kid, as opposed to a football or basketball player, he could see this kid's got mama's boy written all over him. His college future had frat boy written all over it. Jake's a punk. A kiss ass with phony manners. Zip figured Jake's mommy probably still made his lunch which always included an apple, juice box, and a little note telling him how great he was. But Maggie liked the punk so what was Zip supposed to do? He loved Maggie so he supported her to the utmost. But what rubbed him wrong was Jake's fake ass manners.

Every single time the kid was over to Zip's house, when he left, he'd bellow out, "Thank you for having me."

This drove Zip nuts. For one, it sounded so rehearsed and insincere. As if Jake's mom had taught him to repeat the phrase whenever he left someone's house. But Zip really didn't do anything to deserve it. He didn't invite the kid over. Maggie did. He didn't make the kid dinner. He barely offered him a glass of water. It was so silly and Zip knew he was making a big deal of it and being hard on the kid, but Jake was like a trained parrot which annoyed the shit outta Zip. He'd be half-cocked, watching the Golf Channel or some shit and, like clockwork, here came this kid as he exited their home with his phony ass

"Thank you for having me." When Zip NEVER HAD HIM!

Zip saw Jake's truck in front of his house and instantly U-turned the golf cart to avoid any interaction. He needed more beer anyway as his buzz was waning and since he didn't want to go inside to get his car keys he did what he'd done on many occasions. He simply drove his golf cart down the sidewalks, through the business offices' parking lots, across a busy street jammed with commuters driving home from work who were all somewhat bewildered by Zip making them come to a halt as he drove his golf cart in front of them through the bike lane.

Today there seemed to be more cars than usual. More cars meant more eyeballs on him, including cops. He wondered if he'd make another local Next Door post as he'd been written about in the past when he drove his cart on public sidewalks. Some bored hen had seen him and posted something about the legality of it. So he stepped on it. He'd park next to where the shopping carts were returned and run into the Total Wine to grab that night's supply of cold Red Stripes. Then he'd hustle his way back through the same route that got him there. On his way up the sidewalk on this busy commuter street, of course going the opposite direction of the downhill traffic, about halfway up, he saw a cop car heading in the opposite direction. The officer looked over and spotted him.

"Shit!" Zip winced.

Not only was he driving on the sidewalk carrying a case of beer, but he'd also drunk a few beers, hit the vape pen, and swallowed a pill or four, so a DUI was definitely a possibility. He saw the red taillights and turn signal on the cop car flash as it sped past him. The cop changed lanes so Zip was positive the cop was making a U-turn to come after him. All Zip could do was pray he could outrun the cop and that there was sufficient traffic to give him the time he needed to get the hell out of there. He floored the pedal driving faster than he had ever had. He hit a few curves coming off the sidewalk that launched his body upwards and smacked his head on the roof of the golf cart. He swerved into that last left turn he needed to get into his neighborhood and as he flew down his street he hit his garage door opener so the garage would be open and ready.

As Zip flew from the street onto the lip of his driveway, he hit the lips so hard one of his hubcaps popped off and rolled across his lawn but he didn't give a shit. He skidded into his garage and pressed the garage door button. He never confirmed whether the cop was actually following him. He never cared to look out his garage window. His heart was pounding and he just giggled as he popped the top off a fresh cold Red Stripe.

"Damn that was close," Zip muttered.

Of course, Jake drove a tricked-out truck that his rich parents gave him on his 16th birthday. He'd probably scored two goals for his all-white club team that always seemed to get annihilated by lower income clubs full of Hispanic kids. Zip wasn't envious that Jake's truck was nicer than his. He simply wondered why Maggie couldn't see the punk that he saw. Was he raising her right? Zip went into the house and noticed Maggie's door was shut and immediately barged in to see the two of them staring at their phones, not really talking to each other.

"Hello, Mr. Harrison, nice to see you," Jake uttered, in his most disingenuous tone.

"You can call me Zip, Jake. What are you kids up to? Remember, Maggie, your door stays open. My house, my rules."

"Okay, Dad," Maggie replied somewhat sarcastically, as if she'd heard "my house my rules" a thousand times. "We're just hanging," she said.

"I may order pizza if you guys want one."

Zip, with his current buzz and restocked 12 pack, knew it was going to be a pizza night. He'd already concluded that this night would be an evening of between four to five thousand calories of intake to enhance his already established gut. And likely some ESPN, or better yet the Golf Channel, where he could fantasize had he grown up golfing instead of all the time he'd wasted going from one field to another; he could have been a contender instead of the palooka he was now. Lastly, he'd once again enjoy another chance to party with his best friends—Me, Myself, and I. Zip loved those guys and partied with them often.

He thought of making a run to the CVS up the street to flirt with the gorgeous checker. She was half his age and probably looked at Zip like he was her own father, but he was a dreamer. What could he pretend he needed this time? Christ, he already had a drawer full of ChapSticks. So much so he wondered if she thought he had lips as dry as a lizard! He even thought of buying condoms so she'd think he wasn't such a loser.

"Maggie, what kind of pie do you want?" Zip asked.

"We're good, Dad. We're going to In-N-Out."

As Zip plopped himself on the couch, he heard the kids rustling in Maggie's now open-door room as they gathered their things to head past the living room where he was lounging.

"Here it comes." Zip winced to himself as he prepped for Jake's pull on the doll's string exit.

"THANK YOU FOR HAVING ME."

*Goddamnit, kid, can you just be normal or is sincerity not in your DNA?* Zip thought to himself.

"Jake, enough with the 'thank you for having me.' You're welcome here anytime," though he really didn't mean that.

"And Maggie invites you, so I really don't have you as you say. So please, you don't have to say that every time you leave."

Jake was a bit startled. Did his parents send him wayward with their teachings of politeness? As the kids left, Zip handed them a few $20 bills. He felt guilty for admonishing Jake.

"Enjoy your burgers," he said.

Just then his familiar ping chimed in on WhatsApp. The golf boys arranged upcoming tee times and games on the app. Zip saw the list of names chiming in and who was playing tomorrow.

"Fuck, 8:00 a.m.," he growled.

He knew that was early for him. After a night of beers and a few yellow birds, heck noon was early. But he had an inspired buzz and though he knew he'd probably never make it, especially after partying with his besties, he promptly added his name to tomorrow's list. Maggie was driving herself to school.

"Fuck, don't be a bitch. Get up," he said to himself. But inside he knew it was 50/50 at best and with each beer the odds dropped.

Sure as shit, the next morning Zip heard the refrigerator ice machine rattle as Maggie filled her daily water bottle. He couldn't believe it was morning already. His bedroom TV was still on from the night before. His bed covers were strewn everywhere. An empty Ben & Jerry's pint sat on the bedside table. His head was crushed with pain. He looked at his phone.

"Awe fuck," Zip grumbled.

Zip had simply blown another outing with the boys. He didn't know whether they'd be pissed or just chalk it up to another of his frequent occurrences. He felt bad. He convinced himself last night that he'd make it. But that was last night when he was so high he had passed Mars and was heading for Jupiter. So he dragged his ass out of bed, again, and headed for the fridge to grab the only remedy he was assured would fix his hangover. After cracking a cold Red Stripe for breakfast, he smacked himself in the head. It was gorgeous outside and he wanted to golf badly. Then, he thought about Biggs. He pulled out his phone and shot off what he referred to as a "hoper" text. One he hoped would get answered.

*Hey, Biggs, this is Zip, met you at the range. You free to tee it up today?*

Within minutes Biggs replied, *Oh, man, I'm hungover as shit, but yeah some fresh air might do me good.*

*LOL that makes two of us. Think you can be there by noon?* Zip asked.

*Sounds good. Do they allow coolers out there?*

*Like I always tell my kid about her mom, what they don't know don't hurt 'em,* Zip shot back.

*Great! See you then.*

And just like that Zip and Biggs were on for a day of golf.

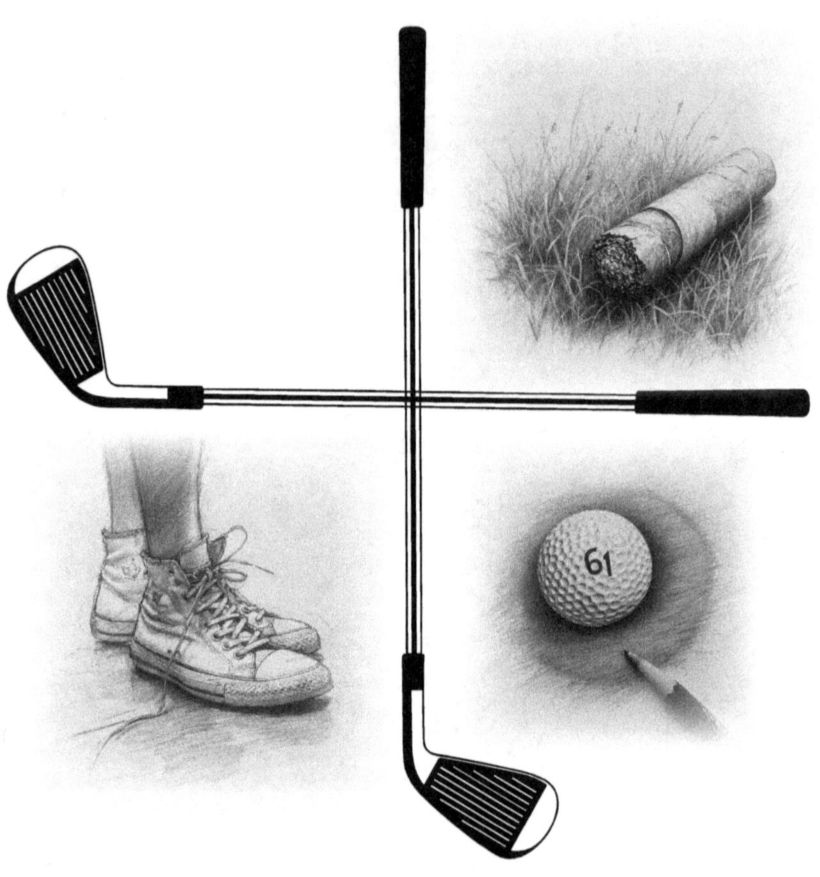

## HOLE #7

Zip arrived at the course around 11:30 a.m. He had plenty of time for some warm-up swings, some putting on the practice green, even some chipping. He was feeling much better after a couple Red Stripes and yellow birds. It was pushing noon and Zip was a tad concerned that Biggs might not show, but at 11:55 a.m. Biggs pulled up. His golf cart blasting music. His cart also had a blue flag attached that signified handicap status and meant Biggs was allowed to drive his cart anywhere on the course or wherever normal carts aren't allowed. This struck Zip as strange. Especially for a guy that was a pro.

"What's with the handicap flag?" Zip calmly asked.

"Oh, my dog bit my ankle so I'm hobbling," Biggs replied.

Biggs walked to the practice green for a putt or three and Zip didn't notice anything hobbled when he walked. In fact, he walked perfectly normal.

"You ready yet?" Zip said sarcastically, as he was already on the 1st tee and Biggs had JUST showed up.

"Of course, let's do this."

Biggs grinned as he pulled a Bud Light from his

cooler in the back of his golf cart and popped the top off. He never turned down his music either amidst the scrutinous eyeballs of every other golfer staring at him from the putting green wondering who the hell this guy was.

"Hey, you got to tuck in your shirt here," Zip explained.

"Oh, that's right, sorry," Biggs said, as he tucked his loosely fit golf shirt into his shorts and approached the 1st tee. Then Biggs, in his beat-up tennis shoes, not golf shoes, took one or two practice swings, put his tee in the ground, and promptly smoked his tee shot straight down the fairway about 280 yards with the most effortless, beautiful golf swing Zip had possibly ever seen.   He walked back to his cart, lit a cigarette, and methodically asked Zip,

"You want to go $100 front, $100 back, and $100 overall?" as if that was normal.

Now Zip liked to bet, no question. He hated losing to his regular golf buddies. It wasn't the money. Zip was as competitive as they come. In fact, Zip often said he'd rather pay his property taxes then have to pay LH or Chewy $10. But $100 a side to a pro? But he didn't want to be a pussy either.

"Easy on the $100, Arnie. We can go $10 a side."

"Roger that." Biggs chuckled.

Next Zip stepped up to the tee and hit a nice shot of his own and walked towards his push cart.

"You want to jump in here?" Biggs asked, referring to his golf cart.

"No, I'm good, I like walking. With this gut I never saw a calorie I didn't want to burn," Zip retorted. "Plus, that cancer stick hanging out of your mouth is nasty. Yes, we're outside but cigarettes travel."

"Suit yourself. You good with music?" Biggs asked.

"Doesn't bother *me* a bit. But something tells me you need it."

Biggs took a long, crackling drag off his cigarette.

"It's always on when I play so I never really thought of it."

The next few hours were everything from bothersome to illuminating. Biggs drove his cart anywhere he wanted. Practically on the greens on some holes. He smoked like a chimney and drank like a fish. He'd place his beer can right next to his ball on the putting green, then place his cigarette on top of the can, and stroke amazing putts sinking balls from any distance though most of his putts weren't generally longer than a few feet. On the 200-yard, par 3 6th hole,

Biggs hit a 6 iron into the green side bunker and Zip, who needed every bit of his 5 wood to hit the green, thought he finally might win a hole.

Biggs practically drove his cart into the bunker.

"Dude, you can't park there! What the F Is wrong with you?" Zip scolded.

"Told you my dog bit my ankle. And this thing has four-wheel drive," Biggs replied, brushing off his new friend.

He disrespectfully flicked his lit cigarette into the sand and hit the most gorgeous, fluffy sand shot that hit a foot next to the pin and almost spun straight into the hole!

"That good?" Biggs smirked, as he picked up his sand covered cigarette and stuck it right back into his mouth. This guy was genius, thought Zip.

"So, what's your story? Why aren't you on tour? Or do you just like kicking the shit out of hacks like me at EV?"

"If I told you, I don't think you'd believe it. And it's kind of embarrassing," Biggs responded.

"Trust me, dude, I'm the poster child for embarrassment." Zip laughed.

"Well, I can play, that's for sure. I've put myself into contention a number of times. It's just that something goes through my head in pressure situations and I choke. My brain goes haywire."

"Well, for one, you don't respect the game," Zip countered. "I thought that was lesson one for a pro. You come out here in beat-up Chuck Taylor high tops, smoke, drink, crank your music. You drive your fucking cart wherever you want. I mean it's kind of ridiculous!"

Biggs was about to tee off on the next hole when he absorbed Zip's dressing down. He turned his music off to respond and Zip assumed he was about to get a dressing down himself for saying such brash insulting comments.

"You know what, you're right. I've always been this way. Instead of hiring a mental coach, maybe I should hire you to straighten me out," Biggs said sarcastically.

"If you did, you'd win the US Open," Zip countered, with equal sarcasm. "Fucking hit already."

Biggs stood over his ball. No cigarette this time. Only a faint crow could be heard cawing in the distance. The peace and quiet was mesmerizing as it hadn't been present all day. Biggs took his long fluid takeaway and promptly hammered his drive a minimum of 300 yards dead right over the houses that lined the 7th fairway, and crashed down onto the adjacent street.

"Paging Dr. Wayright!" exclaimed Zip, as he went on to win his very first and only hole of the day.

"The US Open, huh? Maybe I'll take you up on that." Biggs laughed as his ball soared into oblivion. He cracked another beer, jumped in his cart, turned up the tunes, and off they went.

They reached the 18th hole and Zip looked at the scorecard. He'd definitely lost money to Biggs. But they'd had a nice time getting to know each other.

"Any idea what your score is right now?" Zip asked.

"Not sure. I'm playing well. Even in my Chucks," referring to his shoes.

"It's a little better than that," Zip said. "You make par here and I think you break the course record 62."

"Well, let's make birdie then," Biggs announced.

The 18th hole at EV was a tricky, difficult, par 4 where your tee shot needed to come up short of a pond roughly 250 yards straight away. But the pond also ran along the left side of the fairway and separated the 18th hole from the 1st hole, running in opposite directions. On the right side of 18 was, of course, a row of homes, making an accurate tee shot crucial. The second shot required an uphill 150-yard shot over that pond. So, if you hit a 250-yard tee shot, you could easily reach the pond. But you needed to get your drive close to the pond's edge to make your second shot shorter and easier due to the hill leading to the green. Zip stepped up and laced a 5 wood perfectly to the 240-250-yard mark, not threatening the pond. Zip assumed Biggs would hit an iron, as his driver or 3 wood would surely be wet. But Biggs pulled his driver out. And for a moment, Zip thought Biggs was going to try to carry the pond with at least a 375-yard drive needed to carry.

"Anyone ever play it this way?"

With that, Biggs turned to his left and absolutely tattooed his ball directly through two tall pines just left of the 18th tee box. The pines were like two tall goal posts and his ball split them perfectly through the middle, then faded perfectly over the water that separated holes 1 and 18, and landed softly in the middle of the 1st hole, about 300 yards from the tee box on 18.

"Holy shit, I've never seen anyone play it that way!" Zip exclaimed.

"Creativity," Biggs calmly replied.

Biggs then jumped in his cart and drove around the water onto the first hole fairway right up to his ball. He had about 100 yards left to the 18th green but more tall pines blocked his sight line to the pin. Just then an old timer who lived off the first hole came out onto his back patio and unleashed on Biggs. The old timer's name was Ralph. He was an original homeowner in the EV community as well as one of the golf course's first members. Ralph constantly chewed an unlit cigar because smoking them led to his chronic lung problems. He was well known, well respected, and definitely knew the rules around Eagle Vista CC and wasn't shy about providing them to this new member with the hot shot reputation for disrespecting, what Ralph deemed, his club. Ralph drove an antiquated, beat-up golf cart from the '80s around the course acting like he was some sort of marshal though he had zero authority. But he was a jovial old dude whose health and golf game were clearly behind him so the folks around cut him some slack.

"Get that fucking cart off the fairway!" Ralph screamed. "You ain't supposed to drive on the first fairway! Even if you *have* a blue flag!"

Zip was over on the 18th fairway near his ball, fully expecting Biggs to apologize and get his cart off the grass. Then he heard Biggs respond.

"Fuck you, old man! Who the fuck are you?? Kiss my ass!"

Zip's jaw hit the ground.

"Biggs! Jesus, dude, that's Ralph! And he's right! Get your cart off the fairway!" he yelled, completely startled by the unfolding scene.

Biggs looked back at Zip and said, "Okay, okay, take it easy."

"Hey, are you deaf? Get that fucking cart off the fairway!" Ralph screamed again, as he practically choked on his chewed up cigar.

Biggs turned back at Ralph, shot a glare at him, pulled out a gap wedge, and with no practice swing hit a hasty shot that sailed high over the pines that blocked the 18th green, crashed down with a thud, and spun literally about a foot from the flagstick for a kick in birdie!

Biggs then turned to Ralph, grabbed his nuts and yelled, "SUCK IT, old man. Can you do that?" Then jumped in his cart with the music blaring and drove straight through the pines, which was another off-limits area for golf carts, and up near the 18th green. By this point Zip was pretty flustered by what he had witnessed. Biggs showed zero respect for the club.

"Do I need to putt that one?" Biggs cracked.

"Uhh, no, it's . . . uhm, good," Zip responded sheepishly.

"Course record by one then. Let's grab a beer." Biggs bent over, picked up his ball, and gave a bewildered Zip a fist bump as if nothing had happened.

Zip calmly shook his head, truly bewildered, and said, "Dude, you want to be on tour? You need a shrink . . . badly."

## HOLE #8

The bar at Eagle Vista had tall glass walls that allowed patrons to gaze out over the picturesque holes 1, 10, and 18.  These holes circumvented the large pond that separated them. There was a large fountain in the center of the pond that, when working properly, added to some very scenic views and gorgeous wedding photos. Problem was, like many Eagle Vista amenities, the fountain often broke down and management wasn't exactly prompt at fixing the thing. But, hey, "no negativity" was the theme of the day. Zip's regular golf crew had been in the bar a few hours after they'd finished their earlier round, sans Zip. They sat belly up in the bar as they regularly did, viewing all of the outside activities.

"You see who Zip's playing with?" LH said to the Commish seated next to him, probably enjoying his third or fourth vodka martini with a slice of orange peel attached to the rim of the glass.

Now the Commish was someone that basically knew everyone at Eagle Vista. New and old. He'd spent so much time in that same barstool his ass was imprinted in the faux leather and folks somewhat knew he'd be to the bar at some point each day so they left it unoccupied. This was a good tactic because the Commish could show morning, day, or evening. And some days he'd do all three.  He didn't have a set schedule but, sure as shit, he'd be there looking for an ear to chew on. If you sat next to him, beware. Broach a question on any topic and the Commish could go on for hours without taking a breath. Especially when the topic concerned the Commish personally.

"Yeah, that's that new guy. I've met him," the Commish replied. And, of course, he'd met Biggs.  "He was a pro."

"What's Zip doing playing with him? Did he blow us off to play with him?" LH bitterly asked.

"I bet he did," said the Commish.

See there were no restrictions on who or when you could golf. But the group at EV, although all middle-aged men, had a bit of a clicky dynamic. It was very high school-ish. When a regular group member played with someone outside the group, he was criticized by the other group members. It was odd and immature, but they felt threatened by a new member. Especially one as supremely talented as Biggs. Zip had tried to introduce plenty of new guys to the group. But a few of the old timers would put said new guys through a sort of initiation process where their commitment and behavior earned their way into the group.

It was a ridiculous process and Zip would often tell the elders, "Boys, it's just golf."

"If they want to play then just let them play," he'd argue. But there was a process and any new prospect had to be voted in or out. Zip would love to have Biggs join the group. After all, how often do you get to play with a pro? At anything? But Zip was terrified to have to put Biggs through the group's ridiculous initiation. He could only envision LH telling Biggs to lay up on par 5s or what club he should hit to carry the pond on the 125-yard, par 3 12th. Zip also didn't want Biggs to have to endure another one of the Commish's old baseball brags when he'd announce that he played pro baseball for the Dodgers, never clarifying that it was the Single-A club out of Chico, California.

No, Zip knew his cast of characters well. How could he expose Biggs to Chewy? A wealthy guy, as he was constantly letting the group know, who, of course, bragged he bought Apple before the iPhone and Nvidia before AI. In fact, he earned the nickname Chewy because he was nonstop chatter. His mouth moved so much he looked as if he was constantly chewing. And somehow Chewy's handicap never got above 10 but he never broke 85 at the par 69 Eagle Vista. Chewy's forte was hitting these ugly slice grounders and constantly telling everyone he needed to get to the range. Though he never would and always chose cocktails at the bar as his warm-up. Then it was a few putts on the practice green.

And beware if he actually made a few practice putts because he'd boldly announce, "Oh, look at that, my putter's on fire today," after which he then proceeded to 3 putt every green and miss every 3-footer, or at least the ones he didn't scoop up with the back of his putter while announcing, "That's good."
He did this so often it might have been easier for him to have tattooed, "That's good," on his arm below his shoulder so he could just display his tat under his shirtsleeve instead of actually announcing it.

And talk about a rules Nazi. Because he was terrible, he'd take a ton of mulligans. Not just off the tee but anywhere on the course, including the greens! Some guys started calling him "Take 2 Chew" behind his back of course. He'd constantly better his lie and the winter rules' club length radius, or lift, clean, and place was so liberal to Chewy that he'd find a lie that allowed his next shot to be as beneficial as possible. For him, the one club length local rule often expanded to four or six club lengths. Shots that were originally behind bushes or trees suddenly had clear paths to the green.

Chewy never saw a three-foot curler for par where he wouldn't scoop it up with the back of his putter and proclaim, "That's good."

But, of course, he'd make the hugest stink if a guy didn't, what he judged, mark his ball properly on the green. He'd stand there right next to a guy that was trying to line up a putt and claim the guy cheated after he'd declare the guy placed his ball an inch closer to the hole before picking up his ball marker. The irony was absurd. Chewy would be taking graces and exaggerated club lengths all over the place. But he'd make a huge stink about literally one inch when a ball was marked on the green.

No, there was no way Zip was going to expose Biggs to this nonsense. Especially after he witnessed Biggs accost old man Ralph when Ralph was completely in the right.

Zip and Biggs entered the bar, ordered a beer, and took a table that was strategically a bit of distance from the eyes of the regulars sitting belly up. Zip could feel the curious eyeballs zeroed in on him from the boys as if he chose a new table to sit in the high school lunchroom.

"So, dude, what was that on that last hole? That's Ralph by the way. He's a dinosaur around here, but very well liked. You shouldn't go after him like that," Zip counseled Biggs.

"I give two shits! He was yelling at me about my cart or some shit. I could hardly hear him because of my music. But fuck him."

"I thought pros were required to have some kind of professional demeanor or etiquette at all times?" Zip returned.

"Yeah, well I'm not a pro anymore, am I?" Biggs answered begrudgingly.

"You *just* clipped a course record that's been around more than 30 years. Kinda seems like you still have game," Zip countered.

Biggs put his beer to his lips and, with four big chugs, downed it.
"Yeah, perhaps. Hey, you want another? I'm buying."

Now Zip could drink with the best of them but he'd barely made a dent off of his own beer. "Hold up," he said to Biggs. "I'm buyin'. Besides you crushed me out there so I owe you anyway."

"Nah, don't sweat it. Wasn't a fair fight," Biggs replied, as he rose from his stool to head to the bar for another round.

On his return to the table Zip inquired, "You ever thought of making another run?"

"The tour?" Biggs said. "I mean, fuck, I'd love to but like you said, I need a shrink."

"Maybe you just need the right caddy," Zip said, with a wry smile.

"You got anybody in mind?" Biggs scoffed.

"Well, Dr. Phil isn't available. But I took a lot of psychology classes at Berkeley. I'm also a drug addicted alcoholic, some characteristics I think we share. I think I'd be a qualified candidate. So, let's give it a shot," Zip declared. "I'll straighten your ass out."

"Oh, really?" Biggs snarked. "And how do you suppose you'd do that? I'm losing my shit on an old man just trying to enjoy his afternoon cigar that looked like he was chewing on a wet turd."

"I've maybe picked up a tell," Zip implied. "I'm not positive but . . ."

"A what?" Biggs shot back, interrupting him.

"A tell, like a poker player that gives away his cards without realizing it or a pitcher that tips his pitches before he throws," Zip explained.

At this point Biggs was well on his way to a nice buzz. The eight or nine Bud Lights he slammed on the course along with the few he'd drank at the bar were putting him in his familiar zone. "Well, I basically got no other skills. My brother-in-law offered me a job with his painting business, but I'd just as soon sell insurance."

"Careful," Zip interjected, with a glare.

Zip looked over Biggs' shoulder and could see his crew straining to overhear the conversation he and Biggs were having. In fact, LH was glaring directly at them trying to pick up any tidbit.

"What's Zip saying to that guy?" Zip overheard the Commish ask.

The high school lunchroom gossip vibe was in full effect at the EV bar. True alcoholics rarely listen. They simply wait until whomever they're in a conversation with stops talking or takes a breath before pouncing on the moment to interject their personal nonsense.

"Oh, shit, that's right, sorry . . . you're in the insurance game?" Biggs replied apologetically.

"Pays the bills, but, yes, I think I've noticed something about your game," Zip continued.

"What, dude!? C'mon I got to know!" Biggs excitedly asked.

"Let's agree to tackle this. Work together. I'd rather show you than tell you," Zip replied.

"Zip, if you can fix me, I'm all yours," Biggs said, as he reached out his hand to shake Zip's. "But you gotta tell me why everyone calls you Zip?"

Zip chuckled. "Maybe another time, when I know you better. But, yeah, okay get ready to work then," he offered, with a degree of seriousness he hadn't felt in a long while.

LH was fully enthralled in the handshake he'd just witnessed from across the bar. "Any idea what the F Zip is up to?" LH asked the Commish.

"Kind of looks like they're going to team up somehow," the Commish muttered. "Dollars to donuts, whatever it is crumbles," he said, as he put his fourth martini to his lips for a large tug.

"I'll call you in the morning," Zip said to Biggs, and he walked out the double glass doors towards his golf cart to head home. "Get some sleep."

Zip had a feeling that Biggs was going home to continue drinking just as he would more than likely be beckoning his best friends as well that night. Strangely, he didn't.

PROM

## HOLE #9

Bright and early the next morning Zip was awake drinking coffee at the kitchen counter when Maggie entered to fill her water bottle.

"What the holy heck?" she exclaimed, completely startled that he had  woken up before her.

"What?" Zip responded defiantly. "You got time for breakfast? How does avocado toast sound?"

"It sounds fantastic. Is it Christmas or my birthday? Have I been asleep for months? What are you doing awake, Dad? But sorry, no, I don't have time for breakfast. Had I known you'd be up and offering, I'd a definitely loved some but I got to run. Jake needs me to pick him up this morning."

"Did you ask if his mommy could make lunch for you too, hun?" Zip said, continuing the sarcastic vibe.

"Dad, he's nice. I think he's going to ask me to prom," she said excitedly.

"Prom? When's that? How much will *that* cost me? Or does mama's boy know how to treat a girl?"

"I'll buy my own ticket, Dad!" Maggie barked at Zip. "Or I could wash these dirty ass windows to earn some extra money."

"You *should* be washing windows and vacuuming regardless. When I was your age, I had tons of chores and I didn't get paid!" Zip extolled.

"Dad, if I had a dollar for the amount of times you've told me how hard your childhood was compared to mine or how many chores you had without an allowance, I could afford my own prom tickets," Maggie countered, as she turned from the refrigerator to leave for school.

By this time Zip had reached in his wallet and placed a $20 bill on the counter. "Here, Maggie, get something for lunch. Although $20 probably goes pretty fast at Starbucks. And buy Sophia something. Her mom's hot so maybe she'll put in a good word to her mom for me," he said, with a smile.

"Thanks, Dad. Love you." Maggie snagged the money and said, "Got to go, I'm late."

"Love you too, hun, and learn something today." This was a phrase Zip repeated as much as he mentioned his childhood chores.

He felt fantastic this morning. The coffee tasted great and was a welcomed alternative to Red Stripes. It felt amazing to not be hungover. He pulled out his phone and texted Biggs.

*You ready?*

A few minutes later Biggs responded, *Ready for what?*

*Just get your shit on,* said Zip, meaning his golf gear, *and get ready to get back on tour!* Zip wrote, using an exclamation point and no smiley face or laughing face emojis. *You have a red golf shirt? Wear one.*

*Dude, I grew up watching Tiger win on Sunday. Of course, I have a red shirt,* Biggs answered emphatically. *But WTF do I need one for?*

*Look, as your caddy and mental coach, trust the process and do as I say.*

*Not sure I've hired you to be either of those,* Biggs shot back.

*That's fine if you want to piss away your potential and dominate the dog shit players at Eagle Vista. Let's forget all of this then!*

*Take it easy, Knute Rockne. Fuck I'll put on a fucking red shirt for Christ's sake,* Biggs texted.

*I'll pick you up in my cart in 20 minutes. I'll bring my Bluetooth speaker as well,* was Zip's last text.

Roughly 45 minutes later Zip pulled up in front of Biggs' house as he stood on his front lawn swinging a golf club.

"Sorry, man, my next-door neighbor is Iranian, very nice man, beautiful family. But he was telling me about all the letters he gets from the HOA.  He thinks all of the neighbors that proudly fly their American flags above their garages complain about how he keeps his yard. Which they probably do. It's a bit much, but every house on my block flies the Stars and Stripes in front of it. I'm tempted to fly a Swiss flag just to see how many people I can rile up. But that's a whole other discussion," Zip laughed, explaining his tardiness.

"Dude, your cart has seen better days. That country club quality?" Biggs joked.

"No, but neither are you and, yes, I said red shirt but running an iron over it every couple of years couldn't hurt," Zip retorted.

The sleeve of Biggs' shirt at one time proudly displayed Mission Hills CC. But its current state resembled a road map. All Zip could read was: Mis ills C.  The rest of the sleeve looked like a piece of crumpled tin foil.

"You're lucky it's washed. Where we going, the range?" Biggs queried.

"Something like that, get in."

As they approached the road leading to the driving range, Zip made a left turn down a dirt road adjacent to the range and came to a stop at a large iron gate. This gate connected to a long fence line that separated the range from the huge grasslands where 50 to 60 cows buried their heads in the tall grasses without interruption, oblivious to all the continuous hacking going on just a few yards away. Occasionally, some local teens would aim their 7 iron shots over the fence with the goal of drilling one of these cows. Not many members were involved in PETA. Zip got out of the cart, unhinged the gate, and drove the two of them inside the cow pasture.

"Make yourself useful and go lock the gate." Zip glared. "If one of these cows moseys out of here, we're in big trouble," Zip instructed Biggs.

"Dude, I'm from the beach; I don't do cows. And Jesus that smell!" Biggs complained.

"That smell just might save your ass!" Zip countered.

They drove up a long dirt road maneuvering around the cows and pulled up next to a large, fenced-in cattle pen just off the side of the long fence that separated the pasture and the driving range. A large brand new Ford six-wheel Hennessy truck towing a cattle trailer came over a hill towards them and backed its trailer up next to the pen. A somewhat buffed arm protruded from an overly tight T-shirt and hung out of the Hennessey's window. The arm was attached to a driver wearing a worn straw white cowboy hat with a yellow sweat stain ringing the hat above its bill.

"That's a rad truck," Biggs told the driver.

"We call 'em rigs pards. The name's Elliott. Heard some good things about you." Elliot reached to shake Biggs' hand. Biggs had anticipated a powerful grip but was surprised when a much softer businessman's shake occurred.

Zip intervened. "Biggs, this is Elliot Wallace. He owns all this land and cattle."

"Nice meeting you, sir," Biggs said. "Shit, I didn't realize ranching could be so lucrative."

"Oh, it's not," Elliot answered, with a smirk. "This place cost me thousands to maintain. But I can write off losses and I need write-offs. Don't get me started on the politicians that run this state," Elliott grumbled.

"Nope, we're not going there," Zip proclaimed, as he shot Biggs a "shut the F up" glare. "Just like we have no negativity Wednesday, we also have never politics every day!"

"Agreed." Elliott nodded.

He turned to walk back towards the cattle pen.

Biggs noticed a well-worn tobacco can ring in the back pocket of Elliot's jeans.

"Dude, you gotta dip for me? This early in the morning I could really use one," Biggs asked.

"I don't touch the stuff. Tried it once and it made me barf. I look for used jeans at the Goodwill with Copenhagen tin rings in the pockets," Elliot replied.

"Yeah, Elliott's a real rough and rowdy cowpoke," Zip joked. "I met him years ago. He was just a golf member back then. But he was a VP for NVIDIA. His favorite show is *Yellowstone* so once his stock cashed in, he became a 'rancher,'" Zip sarcastically blurted out.

"That's right! I lift weights in my gym in the mornings, shoot HGH in my butt in the afternoon to stay jacked, and pretend I'm a cowboy all day long. Jealousy will get you nowhere, Zip," Elliot shamelessly admitted.

"Look, Elliot, I knew you when you were a pee on tech nerd. And shitty golfer. Don't big-time me," Zip snarled.

Just then a huge *BANG* hit the back of the metal door of the cattle trailer.

"What the entire fuck was that!?" a startled Biggs yelled.

"That's Rusty, my Brahman bull that I bought to breed these heifers," explained Elliot. "Too bad I didn't do a background on Rusty cuz he'd as soon let you milk him, and by that I mean stroke him, before he'd sow one of these cows. Turns out he was bred to buck cowboys not fuck cows. I've tried everything. Either he's a gay bull or he just don't care about females."

Biggs peeked through the trailer and saw a massive auburn colored bull with horns as thick as the barrel of a wooden baseball bat glaring right at him. Snot bubbles and slobber dripped from his snout.

"Uhm, does Rusty bite?" Biggs asked.

Rusty's head reminded Biggs of the front of a Mack truck. Rusty was 1,800 pounds of pissed off gay bull and as Biggs turned to walk away Rusty started banging his head off the gate of his trailer, agitated to say the least.

Elliott looked over at Zip with a mischievous smile.

"Did you tell this guy what we planned last night? And to answer your question, no he don't bite. But he can do *much* worse."

Zip grabbed a bucket of balls from the back of his cart along with a small artificial turf mat and placed it inside the center of the circular cattle pen. Next, he took out his rangefinder and pointed it at the various posts in the driving range just over the fence.

"Okay, we got 125, 150, and that white one is 180. This will do fine," Zip instructed. "Biggs, grab a wedge and a 7 iron and get over here."

He then pressed his phone and Van Halen's "Panama" started blasting from the Bluetooth speaker Zip had pointed towards the pen. As Biggs entered the pen holding the golf clubs, Rusty's agitation grew louder. "You motherfucker!" Biggs yelled at Zip. "What are you up to? Is this why I'm wearing a red shirt? To piss off this fucking bodacious looking beast?"

"You catch on quick," Zip said, as he emptied some golf balls on the piece of turf and jumped back over the pen's fence to stand next to Elliot on the safe side. "Now hit that 125 pole with your wedge. Elliott, grab that latch on the trailer gate. If Biggs hits a shitty shot, pull the lever and let Rusty at him!"

"What are you fucking talking about, bro? Elliot, don't touch that lever. You're going to get me killed!" Biggs screamed.

"Well, that's up to you, so I'd not miss a shot if I were you." Zip laughed.

Rusty let out a huge, booming, bull moo that roared like it was produced from deep inside his bowels. He trashed his head from side to side and rammed his baseball bat horns loudly off the metal trailer walls.

"Ooh, I think he likes you. It's not the shirt. Rusty's turned on. I think he's attracted to you!" spouted Elliott. "This ought to be fun."

"Well, no it won't cuz I ain't doing it!" Biggs yelled, as he backed away towards the pen's exit gate.

"Just hit a few. Look, there's a method to my madness," Zip screamed back at Biggs.

Biggs took a deep breath and pulled out his wedge. With one eye looking backwards at Rusty and the other eye on the ball placed at his feet, he stroked the first shot gorgeously over the fence. It landed fairly close to the 125-yard post. He exhaled the breath he'd putatively been holding for minutes.

"But you can do better," Zip calmly directed. "Hit the fucking pole like you were doing the other day! Focus! Forget about Rusty!"

"Forget about Rusty? Look at the thing! He's gigantic! He either wants to harpoon me or he wants to jam his giant bull cock up my ass! Maybe if Elliot would get his hand off the fucking lever, I might be able to relax a bit," Bigs pleaded.

"Well, you're the one who decided to dress like a matador," snarked Elliot.

Biggs let another shot fly that just barely missed the bottom of the post but spun about 2 feet away.

"Keep going," Zip demanded.

Biggs proceeded to hit five or six well struck shots, landing cleanly within a 10-foot radius of the post.

"Okay, this is too easy," Zip suggested. "Grab your 7 and let's try for the 180 pole."

Biggs turned a bit to his left and striped a ball that landed 20 yards from the 180-yard post.

"That sucked! Let him go, Elliot!" Zip screamed.

"NO, NO, WAIT . . . I can do better. DON'T touch that fucking lever, Elliot," Biggs begged.

The next shot ascended so gracefully it seemed to hold in the sky just above the post and drop delicately on top of it. He repeated that same shot a few more times.

"Rusty's looking bored," Elliott proclaimed. "Let's make it harder. How about a strong wedge to the 150-yard post?"

Biggs was now so focused out of fear he barely acknowledged Elliot. He pulled another ball to the center of the mat and just before he started his takeaway, Zip pressed his phone and the music abruptly stopped. Biggs stepped away, then readdressed his ball, and in what seemed to be dead silence, shanked a grounder that hopped just through the pen's fence and didn't even reach the driving range fence some 50 yards in front of him.

"Try again, Biggs." Zip yelled. "But you better be on your horse if you do *that* again."

Biggs lined up the ball in his stance. His next attempt was an even uglier hack than the previous one. He whipped his head backwards towards the trailer's door right as Zip sounded off, "Cut him loose!"

And with that command, Elliot yanked the lever and Rusty blasted through the now opened door charging straight for Biggs. Biggs felt a primal reflex overcome his body which was to RUN. As Rusty charged towards him like a freight train, Biggs leaped up onto the fence and threw himself over the top to safety.

"You fuckin' ASSHOLE!!" Biggs exploded.

Elliot and Zip both fell over, laughing hysterically. Zip walked over to calm Biggs who was bent over, his chest heaving with every breath.

"Sure, that was nuts, but I think we found something," Zip said, as he rubbed Biggs on the back with a consoling touch.

"Oh, really?" Biggs replied, half pissed and sarcastically. "Please, enlighten me."

"You can't play in silence. You need constant noise to focus. If you've got music and chaos going on you're a beast, no disrespect to Rusty. But, Biggs, you've got rabbit ears."

"Rabbit ears!? What the fuck you talkin' 'bout, bro?" Biggs countered, with a snickering upper lip.

"I've just been analyzing you," Zip explained, "since the first day we met at the range, to your classy display of sportsmanship with Ralph. If music is blasting, you're as focused on your game as John Daly is at knocking down 30 Good Boys. But the moment the music stops and we play in relative silence, as the game is normally played, you fall apart. Like you can't play. You lose concentration and focus if a stupid bird chirps during your swing. You can't block out the little things because you're hypersensitive to what's going on around you. So you crank music, talk loudly, argue, whatever it takes to help you block out the normal silence in which the game is played. It's classic rabbit ears and we're going to fix that."

"Oh, we are, are we? Thanks, Einstein. Was this a college psych class you took?" Bigs questioned Zip defiantly.

"Hey, I told you I'd fix you, you still in?"

"Yeah, I guess. As long as there's no more fucking Rusty I'm game."

"Hey, Rusty's sensitive! Don't talk about him like that," Elliot cried out.

"Okay, I guess I'm in," Biggs said hesitantly.

"Then I need you ALL in. You think this Rusty experiment was fun?  You ain't seen nothing yet,"  Zip countered. "You've got all the physical tools. Distance, accuracy, short game. If we fix between your ears, we can get you on tour. The qualifiers for the US Open begin in a few months. We're going to implement some unorthodox shit to get you on track. Once we do that we enter the qualifiers. The Open's at Pebble this year. I've walked that place a ton. Used to jump the fence as a kid when it was called The Crosby. Couldn't afford to ever play there when I got older, but I loved to go watch the tourney every year. I haven't always been sober, but I know that place like the back of my hand. We get you in and I'll get you in contention."

"You get me in the US Open and I'll blow Rusty!" Biggs said, with a deadpan expression.

Rusty suddenly kicked the back of his trailer that caused a huge outward dent.

"Kinda thinkin' Rusty just might like that, Biggs." Elliott laughed.

"Listen, no disrespect, but if I can qualify I'm not sure you're the best choice of coach and caddy," Biggs informed Zip.

"I figured out your problem, didn't I?" Zip fired back.

"Well, yeah, but—"

"Well, yeah, but nothing." Zip interrupted. "You buy into my madness and I promise you. Plus I need this, Biggs. My life is dog shit. I need this as much if not more than you. I want Maggie to see her old man in a better light. I want her to be proud of me," Zip said, as he choked up.

"Jeez . . . okay, bro, don't cry on me," Biggs mocked.

"I want in on this," Elliott proclaimed. "We can dial up some new schwag. Hats, visors, shirts. Red, of course. We'll use Rusty's silhouette as our logo. Perhaps we can generate some attention to my ranch and I can start selling organic steaks. You guys tell me what you'll need to finance this venture and I'll cut you a check."

"Maybe I'll play with blue golf balls in honor of yours, Zip," Biggs joked.

"Goddamn, Elliott, that's amazing!" Zip said, ignoring Biggs.

"What do I got to lose?" Elliot scoffed. "Besides, this is par for my course. I can't birth any calves because I bought a gay bull, so I may as well back a golfer that can't play when it's quiet!" he continued, shaking his head in frustration.

"We're about to fix that. Biggs, I mean. Can't help Rusty," laughed Zip.

Biggs and Zip hopped in their cart and bid farewell to Elliot and Rusty. They pulled up in front of Biggs' house and Zip grabbed Biggs by the arm, preventing him from getting out.

"Look, I meant it when I said I need you all in with me. I'm going to try some shit you're going to question big time. Heck, you might even hate me. But if you commit, I promise—"

Biggs interrupted, "Listen, Zip, you said how you needed this? I can't tell you how much I feel the same. I'll walk naked through the grocery store if it'll help me get on the tour."

"I hadn't thought of that but you're close. I'll pick you up in the morning. We are going on a field trip."

"Where?" Biggs curiously asked.

"I know the women's golf coach at Cal. They practice at a club in the Berkeley Hills. We're going to the driving range. You got a bathrobe?" Zip asked.

"Uhh . . . yeah, but—"

"Remember, don't question me," Zip interrupted Biggs abruptly.

"Okay then . . ." Biggs muttered curiously. "I'll see you in the morning, in my robe." At this point Biggs was fully miffed at whether he should have agreed to this partnership with Zip.

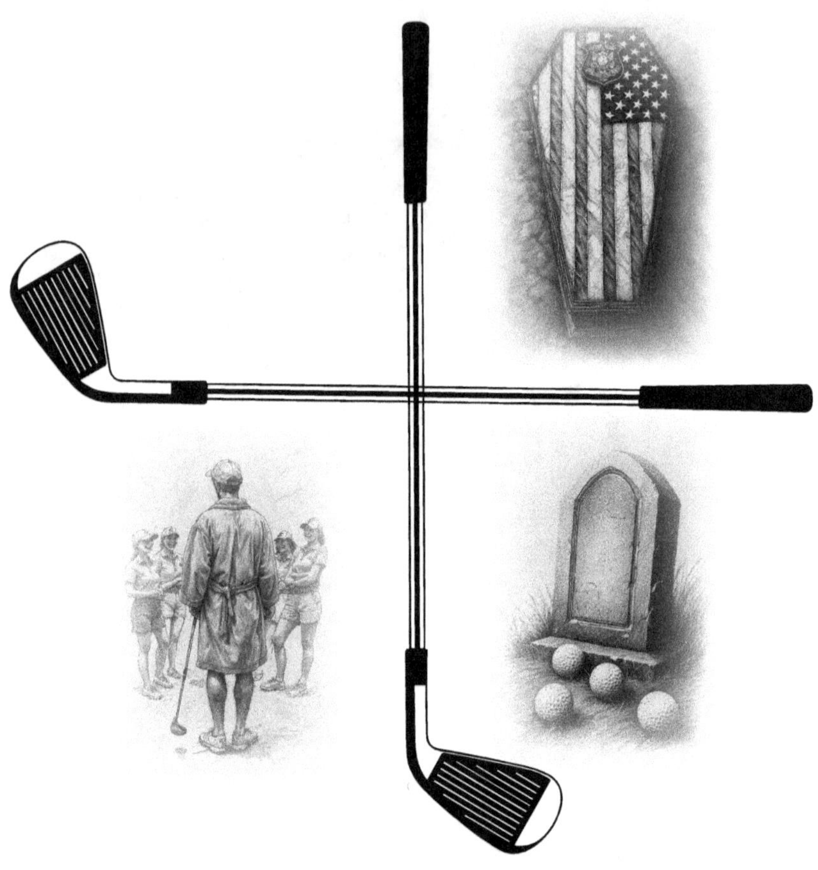

## HOLE #10

When they drove into the parking lot of the lavish Euclid Gates Country Club in the Berkeley Hills, Zip marveled at the huge white columns on opposite sides at the club's entry. Uniformed attendants quickly descended the wide staircase as Zip's car pulled up eager to unload their golf bags.

"We're not playing today, fellas," Zip said to an attendant, "just here to hit balls at the range. Coach Stevens invited us. Is she here?"

"Yes, sir, the team's been hitting only a few minutes. Can I load these onto a cart and drive you both up there?" one of the eager attendants asked.

"That's okay, we got it," Zip replied and he loaded Biggs' bag on the back of the golf cart.

"Only one of you has a bag, sir?" the attendant asked.

"Yeah, I'm his caddy.  Where's the locker room? We need to change," Zip continued.

"The men's locker room is just on the right after you enter at the top of the stairs. Your cart will be waiting here."

"Thanks, kid."

Zip handed the kid roughly three $1 bills folded

up to look like more. It was the only cash he had on hand and folding them to look like a generous tip was an old trick Zip used often with the hundreds of bartenders he'd bought drinks from. The kid was grateful, but Zip would later be the target of some fairly poignant, personal insults by the attendants in the cart barn.

Biggs swung his backpack carrying his bathrobe over his shoulder as Zip directed him to the locker room. Once inside the locker room Zip reached into a plastic grocery bag he'd been carrying and pulled out a lime green piece of fabric and flung it at Biggs.

"Here you go, put this on."

Biggs unraveled the fabric and from his two index fingers dangled a lime green mankini made famous from the beginning of the movie *Borat.*

"Jesus H. Christ! You've got to be kidding me?!"

"Let's go, buddy. US Open," Zip replied flatly.

After the encounter with Rusty, Zip reminded Biggs he said he was "All In." Biggs simply shook his head in disbelief, peeled off his clothes, and proceeded to strap on the mankini, that left little to the imagination.

"Jesus, was one of your parents a grizzly bear?" Zip gasped, as he noticed the abundance of hair patches protruding from Biggs' back.

"Yeah, my Hungarian grandmother had a mustache and smoked two packs a day. Lived till she was 102. Too bad I'm not as handsome as you are!" Biggs sarcastically snapped back.

"Touché." Zip chuckled.

"So hence the robe?" Biggs realized. "Do I at least get to wear it, PLEASE?" he pleaded.

"Of course, you can wear it . . . until we get to the range."

The first thing Biggs heard as they pulled up to the driving range was the incredibly loud cracking sounds of golf balls being smacked from the various hitting bays stretched out along the range. At each bay, perhaps 15 to 20 in all, was a member of the Cal women's golf team, systematically striping ball after ball. Their coach, a very athletic looking, beautiful blue-eyed blonde woman walked behind each of the team members evaluating their swings and performance. The team was all business. Sharply dressed in their colorful blue and gold Cal golf attire. Heads down. Grinding through a routine practice.

"Hey, Allison," Zip said to the coach, extending his hand, "thank you so much for having us out here."

"This the guy?" Allison asked flatly.

Allison was all business and barely acknowledged the grown man wearing a robe and golf shoes in front of her.

"Zip has told me some good things. And that you have some issues. Hopefully my girls can help," she said. "Grab a mat, lose the robe."

"Come on, Zip, please don't do th—" Biggs begged.

Zip cut off Biggs mid-plead. "You heard the coach. Lose the robe!"
He poured a bucket of balls into the ball holder adjacent to the hitting bay.

Biggs slowly, nervously, peeled his bathrobe off his shoulders. At this point every girl on the team had stopped what they were doing and had all turned to see just what in the world was happening. Who was this dude getting ready to hit balls next to them and what was with his outfit? they wondered.

Before Biggs' robe hit the ground he heard a chorus of whoops and whistles. The mankini glistened brightly in the warm sunshine leaving little to the imagination. Biggs grabbed his 7 iron.

"Fuck it," he said. "Let's do this." He then started smoking golf balls into the driving range's blue sky.

"Didn't realize it was *that* cold!" one of the girl's zinged almost immediately which produced a huge roar from the rest of the team.

"You need a few more balls, sir?" another girl mocked. "You seem to be missing a few."

"Come on, pal. Head down. Stay focused. Center of the club face," Zip demanded.

Biggs kept his head down, practically wallowing in embarrassment, as he hit ball after ball. At this point the sun was roasting the skin beneath Biggs' hairy shoulders. But the red burn could not compare to the deep red blush his cheeks displayed. The girls, to say the least, were also a bit confused at what they were witnessing.

"Girls, gather up. This is Biggs," said Coach Allison. "He's making a run for the tour, but he's got some concentration issues we're trying to help him with. Let's make a semi-circle around him so we can see if he has any flaws . . . in his swing, that is."

On cue, the girls simultaneously burst out laughing.

"What are you doing to me, Zip?" Biggs cried, fully flustered.

"Look, you gotta block all this shit out. And hit great shots. We need you to microfocus."

"Micro?" one of the girls quipped. "That feels like an appropriate term," which unfailingly drew another eruption of laughter.

"This puts a whole new spin on gripping your putter," yelled another team member.

Biggs by now was feeling oblivious to his embarrassment. He started to care very little about the comments and the laughter and methodically and repetitiously hit ball after ball. His shots sailed into the air, gloriously on target, while the strap of his mankini disappeared up his butt crack and encased his package. He was in a zone. He worked through every club in the bag. By the time he pulled out the driver, the girls were cheering loudly with every strike. His drives started smacking the fence halfway up at the end of the range some 280 to 300 yards away.

"Get you some!" one of the girls yelled, as a ball sailed over the net into the trees beyond the range.

"Attaboy, Biggs! Get you some of that!" yelled another girl.

The team continued to yell words of encouragement as Zip sat on a bench taking it all in.

"Okay, Biggs, you can put your robe back on," Zip said, as Biggs got to his last few balls.

Biggs lifted his head and realized most of the girls had gone back to their own mats and returned to their practice. He was so focused he hadn't realized he was basically alone at his hitting bay.

"Show's over," Zip said.

"Thank God," Biggs replied. "I get your madness, Zip. My focus and concentration suck. I'm sure I've given these girls a hell of a memory, so let's get the fuck out of here dude."

"Yeah, we're good," Zip answered. "Plus, we got to go anyway. Our short game drill starts at the next location."

"Meaning what exactly?"

"You'll see, get dressed."

They jumped in Zip's truck and proceeded to head even further up into the Berkeley Hills. They came to a four-way stop and Zip signaled to make a left onto a secluded two-lane road lined with huge eucalyptus trees that led into the foothills. In the middle of the intersection stood a motorcycle police officer who extended his arm directing Zip to wait while he waved his other hand signaling the oncoming traffic to turn right up into the long canyon road. Biggs was intrigued by the long procession of single file police on motorcycles making the turn. Their red and blue police lights flashed but there were no sirens. The procession was followed by an even longer, single file line of police cruisers and SUVs doing the same. The procession seemed endless until towards the end came a few limousines with blacked-out windows, followed by a long black hearse. A few more police motorcycles followed behind. Zip and Biggs sat at this intersection for at least ten minutes and watched this solemn motorcade pass in front of them. Finally, after the last bike passed, the traffic cop put his helmet on, jumped on the motorcycle next to him, and sped up the roadway.

"Whoa, dude, what happened?" Biggs asked.

"They're telling folks this young cop was killed doing a home welfare check. But I know a guy close to the situation who says the young cop walked into his house and found his wife in bed with a fellow veteran cop. The younger cop lost his mind at the sight of a fellow officer, and someone he knew pretty well no less, in his bed bangin' his wife! So he went ape shit. Pulled out his gun while the cop in the bed jumped up and pounced on the younger one's back, stark naked, and choked the young cop out. He died. I guess the veteran cop that was doing the banging is the Oakland mayor's right-hand man and is on the mayor's security team. So, they're obviously trying to keep it under wraps. Only a few people know what really happened."

"And how the fuck do you know then, Zip?" Biggs asked. "You seem to know a lot of people."

"I wrote policies for a few of these high-ranking cops. Known 'em for years. Watched them grow through the ranks to high levels."

"You never cease to amaze me, Zip."

"Sit tight. You ain't seen nothing," Zip said, as he made a left turn to follow the motorcade up the hill that passed beneath a decorative archway that read: Emerald Hills Cemetery.

"What are we doing, dude?" Biggs queried in a curious, annoyed tone.

"Our greenskeeper at EV, Chris, does weekend work on the grounds here. He's sectioned off an area for us to practice short game."

Chris wasn't the brightest bulb. He had an inbred look to him and after conversing with him a person could be convinced he snorted fertilizer. In fact, his favorite thing to do was snorkel through the various polluted ponds at Eagle Vista looking for golf balls on the bottoms.  These ponds were so brown and full of fertilizer runoff and pesticides that, although shallow, no one could see the bottom. Chris was often seen choking and spouting globs of this brown toxic water through the top of his snorkel.

"I guarantee you he glows radioactive green when he sleeps," Zip said to Biggs.

They pulled into the cemetery and turned to the right as the police procession weaved to the left. All of the cops then proceeded to walk to and around an uncovered grave adorned with huge flower reefs in a poster size photo of the deceased officer. An American flag draped over his casket. His widow and two small kids were seated in the front chairs. Her lover, the mayor, and hundreds of law enforcement all wore their dress blues with the obligatory sunglasses and surrounded the casket. Zip insinuated that the lover and mayor needed the sunglasses to hide their disingenuous sorrow and embarrassment.

"Nothing like good old taxpayer infidelity," he smirked.

He parked the truck along the cemetery grounds some 50 yards from the funeral. Within a definite eyeshot of its mourners.

"Grab your 56 and 60 degree wedges," Zip instructed Biggs. He then dropped a shag bag full of golf balls on the well-manicured grass.

"Zip, no! The college girls were humiliating enough, but this is going to get us fried!"

"Look, I know the *real* reason they're out here," Zip countered. "If they even say a peep to us the mayor and his minions go down! Now, see that tombstone over there?" Zip motioned to a small white, unassuming, rectangular stone some 50 yards away. "I want to see some flops with the 60, bump and runs with the 56. We're here to practice. If you keep resisting, I'm going to make you put the mankini back on. FOCUS!" Zip barked.

And with Zip's urging, Biggs started to chip balls. Every couple of balls he'd peek up. The first thing he noticed was the sound of the beautiful bagpipes being played suddenly mimicking the shriek of a female cat in heat as the bagpiper's jaw dropped in disbelief and the air in his bag escaped. He also noticed that every single finely dressed police officer was glaring at him. But they all had sunglasses on, so Biggs pretended they weren't looking in his direction. He decided to just keep his head down, make clean chips, and figured the sooner he got to business, the sooner they'd get the hell out of there. One after the other Biggs started pummeling the various tombstones Zip instructed him to hit.

"See that one right there? That says Jerry Harrison, died 1986. I want you to bludgeon it with 56 degree bump and runs," Zip sternly instructed.

"Dude, I can't do that. It's better if I don't see the names. This is completely disrespectful. I can't even imagine what these people are thinking of us."

"BLUDGEON IT!" Zip demanded. "In fact, forget the other ones. I want you to just engrave that one with Titleist imprints."

"Jesus, dude, what's with Jerry Harrison? He owe you money or something?" Biggs asked.

"Nope, that's my piece of garbage old man. Drunk left us when I was ten. Tried coming back into my life when he thought I might make the NFL, which basically tells you what a delirious drunk he was. But he left my mom and me high and dry. Go on. Rattle his cage. Wake him up like he used to do to us when he'd come home hammered."

"Okay, you're the boss," Biggs said reluctantly.

He alternated wedges and followed Zip's instructions. He hit flops, runners, line drive punches. There were spinners that bounced and spun, as well as bullets that smacked square off the face of the stone. It was simply a magnificent display of short game artistry.

"Nicely done, Biggs!

The old man definitely knows we're here!" Zip shouted in joy.  The funeral proceeded to go about its business. Even when the 21-gun salute rattled every bird out of the cemetery's surrounding trees, Biggs methodically went about his incredible display of precision short game directed at the tombstones, specifically at Zip's father's, which was somehow therapeutic for him. After about 45 minutes and what was likely 1,000 glares of outrage and lividity, Zip grabbed his ball picker and, just like that, said,

"You're good, we're done."

They started picking up the balls that were sprinkled around the grounds. Chris the groundskeeper was waiting and watching at the top of the hill. As Zip and Biggs briskly walked past him towards the truck, Zip thanked him and slipped a $100 bill in his hand.

"Let's get the fuck out of here before this thing is over," Zip said, motioning towards the funeral. "These cops look ready to pounce."

"Please tell me we're done for the day. I need a fucking drink," a clearly frazzled Biggs demanded.

The ride home was quiet, to say the least. Zip was in deep thought reviewing Biggs' magnificent abilities while also trying to come up with some new exercises to work on. He also reminisced about his childhood. He wondered if he could ever get over the trauma he endured at the abuses of his father. Having Biggs hammer his father's tombstone with a few dozen golf balls was not the most mature way to erase his past, but he chuckled to himself because it definitely felt good. Deep down he knew it wasn't a healthy manner of therapy.

Biggs' silence, on the other hand, was a cross between being baffled and shocked. He contemplated Zip's methods but was too bewildered to speak about it so he sat silently in the passenger seat with a blank stare across his face. At one point Zip reached for the volume knob on the stereo and muttered something about liking a particular song, but Biggs just then realized he hadn't heard any music up to that point. He felt he was sitting in complete silence. Maybe there *was* something to these zany tactics Zip forced him to complete, he thought. Somehow he had been able to completely block out the driving range embarrassment and silently focus on simply hitting golf balls square on the club face. And he knew that every single cop at that funeral would have tased him if they could have, but somehow he was able to block out that distraction and continue to practice. Was there some validity to this rabbit ears concept?

Zip broke the silence. "I'll see you in the morning. Be ready to work."

They were already back home in front of Biggs' house. He was so dumbfounded, and somewhat stupefied, in his reflections of their day that he hadn't realized they had driven all the way to his house.

"Do you want to tell me what all that was about?" Biggs politely asked.

"All what was about?" Zip tried deflecting but he knew the topic. "My father? It's not unique. Lots of people have fucked up parents. In fact, so many do it kinda gets old hearing about it so it was what it was. He wasn't raised right, so he just continued the path of destruction with his own family. He was a drunk and guess what? I am too. It's in me. I couldn't please him and when I kept getting hurt in football instead of showing any concern, he laid into me even harder. Like I wasn't tough enough and somehow I had caused my knee and shoulder to get torn to shreds. So, yeah, I needed you to hammer his gravestone with balls cuz I woulda missed every try!" Zip said, belting out a lighthearted laugh.

"Okay . . . Roger that. Can only imagine what's in store for tomorrow." Biggs shrugged as he stepped out of the truck and grabbed his golf bag from the back.

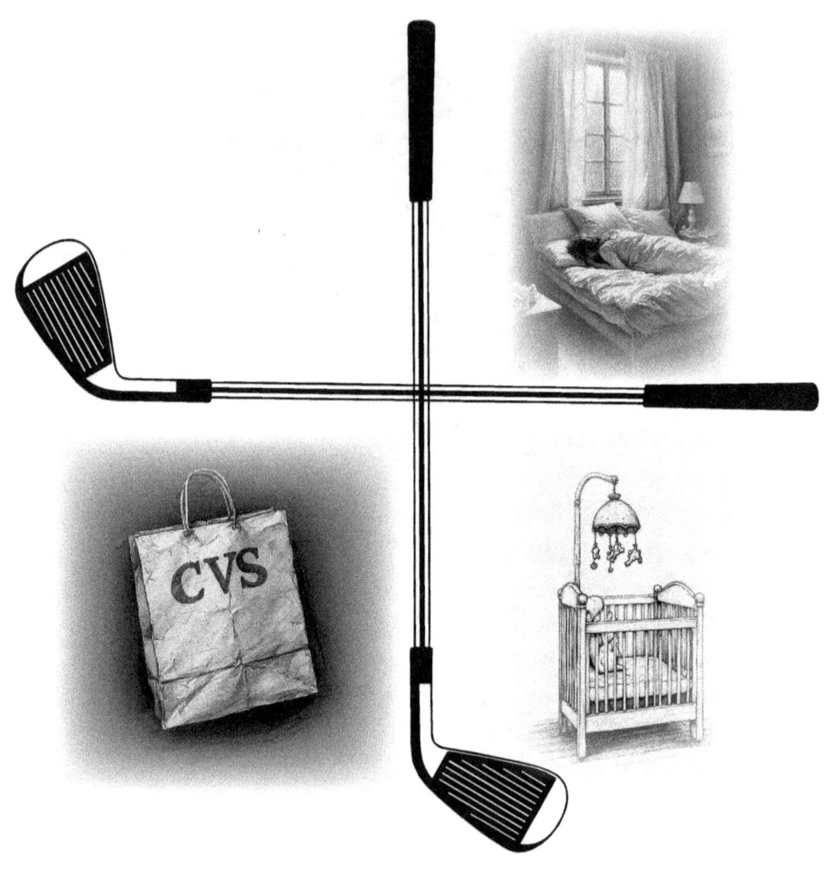
CVS

## HOLE #11

The next morning Zip pulled up to Biggs' place before 8:00 a.m. He was a little surprised Biggs wasn't out on the front lawn swinging a club and getting loose, as he had done the previous encounters when Zip picked him up. Zip walked up to the front door. Knocked a few times. Then rang the doorbell.

"Where is the punk?"

He checked his watch and thought perhaps Biggs was in the backyard warming up so he opened the side gate and went around back. Biggs wasn't there either. The sliding glass door leading into the house on the back porch was unlocked so Zip slid it open and poked his head in the kitchen.

"Biggs?" he called. "You here?" There was no answer. "This motherfucker better not be hungover in bed," he murmured.

He slowly walked down the dark hallway towards the only bedroom in what was a somewhat cluttered, small, dimly lit home. He gently tapped the bedroom door open and saw a figure under the bed covers. A nightstand next to the bed had a few prescription bottles on top of it next to a lamp without a shade. The bedroom curtains were pulled together so tightly that very little light came in.

"All right, what the fuck you doing in b—" Zip blurted out, just as a woman peeked her head out from beneath the covers startling him. "Oh shit. I'm so sorry! I was looking for Biggs."

"No, it's fine," the woman said in a gravelly, raspy voice. "He'll be here any minute."

She pulled the covers back over her head leaving Zip feeling extremely awkward just standing there in the bedroom. He quickly turned to go back through the kitchen when he heard Biggs come through the front door.

"Zip?" Biggs called out. "Sorry, man, I had to run to the store real quick. Come on, I'm ready. Just need to give this to my wife."

He slipped past a speechless Zip while carrying a CVS Pharmacy bag. He went into the bedroom for about thirty seconds and hurried right back out.

"Let me grab my sticks from the garage."

Zip turned to Biggs after they jumped in the golf cart. "I am *so* sorry.  I thought you lived alone. Are you married? You never mentioned anyone."

"I didn't?" Biggs answered. "Yeah, that's Jessica.

Sorry she's been out of sorts lately. Spends a lot of time in bed unfortunately."

"No worries, man. I just hope I didn't freak her out," Zip replied.

"No, no, not at all. I don't even think she knew it was someone else other than me. She's, well, shit, I guess we're going to get pretty close these next few months so I may as well tell you." Biggs was struggling with his words. "Uhm, we've been married a few years. It's been rough."

"Listen, you don't have to tell me anything, Biggs. It's not my business," Zip interrupted.

"No, actually it kind of is in that the situation has something to do with my game, I think. Not until you mentioned this rabbit ears thing did I even consider it. We've been married almost five years. We had a daughter." Biggs started to stammer and fight back a few tears. "Fuck it never goes away, the hurt. But we had a daughter that was born with . . . well, her windpipe wasn't developed correctly so right away the doctors, shit it seemed like an army of them, had to insert a breathing tube and she was put on a respirator. We couldn't bring her home from the hospital for months. We basically lived in the intensive care ward. 24-7 we monitored her breathing. The doctors and nurses were incredible. My wife was . . . I can't explain how amazing she was.

"We named her Carly. Just the tiniest little thing but damn she was tough. After a couple three to four months she was a bit out of the danger zone. Strong enough to come home. But Carly still had to be connected to the breathing tube. A year is what they told us before she needed corrective surgery to fix her windpipe. It was just too dangerous to do this type of surgery until she was at least a year old. So Jessica and I were like hawks making sure she was okay and breathing. We had a night nurse but I don't think either of us really slept more than a few hours a day. Month after month. Felt like we checked on her every minute. Sure, the nurse was there to help but we just wouldn't take our eyes off Carly.

"Then our insurance started to run out and soon we lost the nurse. My mother-in-law lived close so she came and helped. Carly was getting stronger. Jessica even started to persuade me to go back to the Korn Ferry Tour and trust me, we needed the money. But I just couldn't leave them. Our savings was running out and we were living on credit. But finally we felt Carly was strong enough and with Jessica's mom to help, I could go out and try to make some money back on the tour."

At this point tears were rolling down Biggs' face. He was clearly struggling to tell this story.

"Listen, please. You don't need to tell me anymore. I can see how difficult this is. I can't even imagine your pain," Zip said, putting his hand on Biggs' shoulder.

"It's okay. It's actually good to talk," Biggs said. "So I was in Boise playing a tournament, doing pretty well. In the top three, actually heading into the final round. This was just over a year ago. My mother-in-law had Covid and Jessica didn't want her in the house, so she convinced her mom and me that she was fine to watch Carly by herself until I got back."

"Oh, Biggs . . . this is none of my . . ." Zip said, anticipating where this was headed.

"Yeah, Jess had been up for like 72 hours straight. You see if Carly rolled over or somehow the breathing tube was dislodged or she grabbed it . . . We'd wrap her snug in her blanket to restrain her arms at night but, man, we just would listen all night long to make sure she was breathing. Night after night. Day after day. Just living in silence listening to the ventilator and listening to Carly. So Jessica had been up way too many hours all by herself and she, well, she fell asleep. It wasn't her fault. She just fell asleep. When she woke up somehow the breathing tube was pulled out. Carly might have rolled over, but she wasn't breathing. Jess did everything she could to resuscitate Carly but she hadn't been breathing a while by that point. There was nothing we could do."

"Biggs, I'm so, so sorry, man," Zip said. Tears were now running down his cheeks as well.

"Jessica's been a mess. I came straight home from Boise. Didn't finish the tourney obviously. I only started playing again recently and that's because Jess forced me to get out of the house. I know losing my shit on that old man Ralph is a result of all the bullshit. Jess is so depressed; all she wants to do is sleep. She can't bear to be awake. That bag you saw me carrying was sleeping pills and Xanax. I know she's got to come out of it but she won't. She won't get help and she barely eats. What you saw, Zip, is what I've been living with for over a year. I'm so crushed I can't explain it. I've lost a baby *and* a wife.

"We used to have so much fun together. I met her just after college. I was trying to go pro and she worked at this crappy little driving range where I'd practice. Jess had game too. We'd go play rounds together and we battled each other. Man, she was so beautiful. She used to laugh so much but trust me, when it came to her golf, she was all business and would compete. When we were first married, before Carly, we lived in a tiny studio that stunk from the waft of our golf shoes we left by the front door. It was hard. We were broke. We basically survived on Cheerios. Not the brand name ones either. The crappy ones that were called toasted oats or something that we'd sweeten with the free sugar packets from Starbucks. But we were totally happy. When life got really hard, we had this phrase—B-A-T— that we'd constantly say to each other. After bad rounds or when we didn't have enough money for bills. We'd keep telling each other BAT, BAT.

"What's BAT mean?" Zip asked.

"It's dumb but it stands for "Biggs Are Tough." When shit got bad, that's what we'd say to each other to give us hope that we could handle it, get through it. It hasn't been working lately though. The only small relief I've felt, as embarrassing as it's been, has been working with you and our project."

"Goddamn, this is heartbreaking. But you said something earlier about this tragedy contributing to your rabbit ears?" Zip asked.

"Yeah, I think I can't stand the silence. It just puts me in that world where Jess and I were. Sitting in a silent house all those days and nights just listening. Listening for breathing. Never really having the TV on or music. Nothing that would prevent us from hearing if Carly was breathing. And now my house is even quieter. Jessica just sleeps and I feel so awful I don't want to disturb her. I know it's not healthy, but we're devastated. So, if I'm playing and there's noise I feel relaxed, I feel great. The silence takes me down to a dark place. I can't stand the anxiety I feel. But I'm enjoying working with you, Zip, like you can't imagine. I need you. I need what we're doing. That's why I haven't argued or resisted one bit with your stupid fucking drills you're making me do."

Biggs was able to chuckle a bit as he wiped away some final tears. "We're going to do this, Biggs."

Zip looked Biggs straight in his eyes. He had a dead serious, fierce look about him. He hadn't experienced this powerful emotion in as long as he could remember. He could almost feel his heart welling up and bursting out of his chest.

"We're going to do this!" he repeated emphatically.

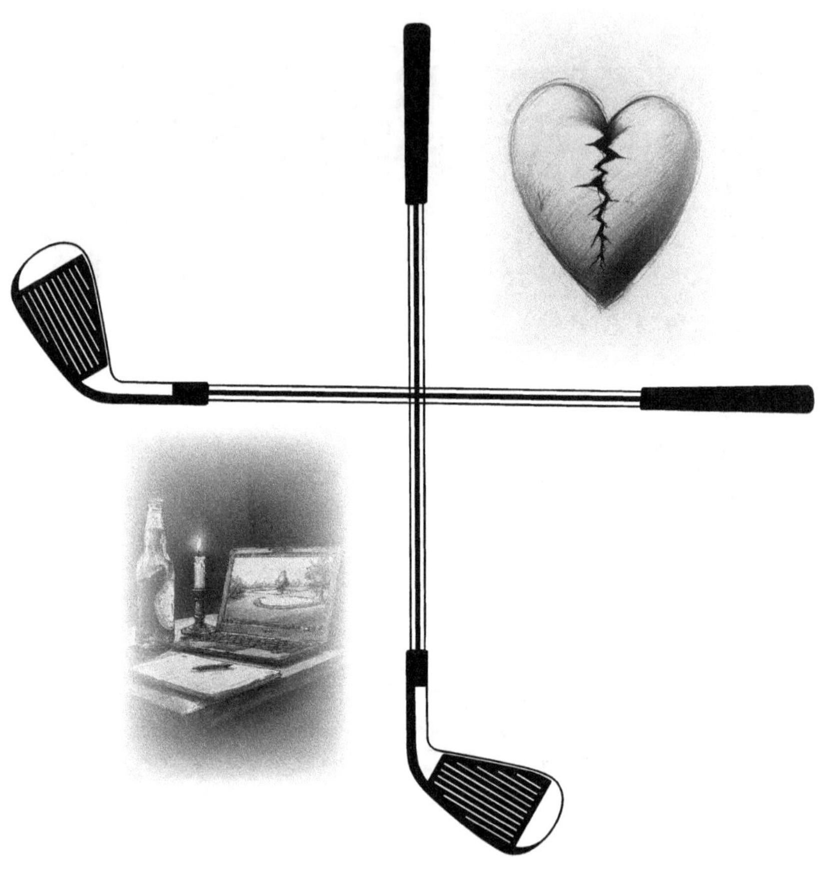

## HOLE #12

Zip pulled into his driveway and immediately noticed Jake's truck wasn't parked in its usual spot out front.

"Oh, sweet! That punk's not here," he muttered to himself. He walked through his garage into the hallway. Maggie's door was closed and no lights showed through the cracks at the base of her door. The hallway lights and the kitchen lights were off as well. Only her water bottle sitting on the kitchen counter gave any indication Maggie was even home.

"Maggie?" Zip asked, as he lightly knocked on her bedroom door. "You in your room?" To which he got no answer.

"Honey?" he repeated.

"Yeah," uttered Maggie in an unusual tone that Zip could barely hear. He knew something was wrong.

"Can I come in, hun?"

Zip always asked permission from Maggie if he could enter her room. She was a grown teen and he respected her privacy. He felt she deserved that kind of respect and the small gestures were examples of his love for her.

"Are you sick, Maggie?" Zip asked, as he entered Maggie was in bed. Her bed covers and blankets were pulled over her head. She was not one to nap, so Zip assumed she had to be sick to be in bed at this time of the day. Maggie sat up, tears rushing down her cheeks. Zip's stomach sank. He hated seeing Maggie upset. He would do anything to ease any type of pain she felt and if she was suffering, he physically felt the hurt as well. Maggie's lower lip was noticeably quivering. She could barely speak.

"Jake broke up with me." And she burst into even more tears.

"Oh, sweetie," Zip said.

He sat down beside her on her bed and put his arm around her. Maggie buried her head into Zip's shoulder and chest and just started bawling. All he could do was hold on to her and try to give her support and comfort as he rubbed her back.

"What happened, did he give you a reason?"

At this point Maggie was really crying and couldn't answer because her sobbing prevented any words. Zip felt crushed for his daughter. At the same time he was pissed off at anyone that could hurt his daughter like this. He wanted to throttle Jake.

"Take a breath, honey. Tell me what happened," he consoled. Zip grabbed a few tissues from a box on her bed table. They hadn't had a close embrace like this in a long time. Sure, they hugged every now and then but like any parent-child relationship, levels of affection had dissipated over the years as Maggie grew up. But, in this instance, it was clear she needed her dad. She was hurting and if Maggie hurt, Zip hurt.

"He just said"—she tried getting her words out between sobs—"he said he feels like his school and soccer are suffering cuz he's spending too much time with me. Like he needs to concentrate on his grades and trying to get a soccer scholarship."

"That little fucking mama's boy! He ain't tough enough to get any kind of college scholarship. I guarantee you his mom had something to do with this," Zip snarled. "She probably wasn't getting the attention she needed from him so she blamed you for him just being average at soccer."

Zip wasn't wrong. He played college sports and knew the mental toughness it took to play. Any sport. Some spoiled suburban kid like Jake didn't have the desire or hunger that's needed. He'd been told his whole life how good he was in the small community they lived in but the next level is a whole different story.

"Dad, my stomach hurts so bad. I don't know what to do," Maggie cried. "We were supposed to go to prom!"

"I know, hun. I know how much it hurts. Trust me, I know." He just held her for what seemed to be about an hour. They just sat there together in Maggie's dark room. Zip held his daughter and was so grateful he had this opportunity to be there when she hurt like this.

"Maggie, mark my words, he *will* regret this. It's going to hurt. You've never experienced something like this before and it's going to hurt like you never think this pain will go away. But believe me he will regret this. And time, time is the only thing that will make your pain go away. It sucks because that fucking clock just seems to go *so slow* when you're hurting. You are a sensitive girl and this kind of shit hurts sensitive people twice as hard. But the time will pass and I promise the hurt will get better.

"When you start feeling good and get over him, that's when that punk will start coming back. He'll never find anyone as good as you and he will realize it and start missing you like crazy. But the weird thing is, even though you hurt so bad right now, when he does try to come back, and he will, you'll be over him. You won't want him back. You'll remember all this pain and hurt you felt, and weirdly, you won't give a shit about him."

All Maggie could do was look at Zip with welled up tears and nod her head. She trusted her dad.

"He's going to try to text you and call you, hun. You go radio silence on that asshole. Okay? Promise me you won't respond."

"Okay, Dad, I promise," Maggie replied, in a voice drained down to a whisper.

A few hours passed. Zip was watching TV and heard Maggie drag herself from her room. She was exhausted by her emotions. She lay down on the couch and put her head on a pillow Zip had put on his lap so she could watch TV with him. He draped a blanket over her. Maggie hadn't watched TV and cuddled with her dad in many years, but she was just in a state that she needed his support and he was more than willing to be there for her.

"What about school, Dad? He's in my first period English class."

"Let me tell you about Nicole," Zip said. "I was in love with Nicole my senior year. She liked me, too, but she broke my heart just like Jake did. The worst part was she started dating a guy that lived on my street! A real gearhead that had engine parts all over his front yard. Total loser family. Not sure if the term white trash is too harsh, but they fit the profile. I couldn't believe Nicole liked this guy. We would still hook up at parties on weekends. I just loved her *so* much. But, like clockwork, every Monday after we'd hooked up, as I drove home late after football practice, sure as shit her car would be parked in his driveway next to all the engine parts. It just used to CRUSH me!

"Time passed so slowly and that stupid clock seemed like it took forever, but the time did pass and eventually I got over her. And without a doubt she tried getting me back but I'd driven past his house, seen her car out front one too many times, hun. I was done. This will happen to you too. You walk in that class tomorrow morning, chin up high, big smile on your face. I don't care how you do it, but fake it if you have to. But you smile. You act like you're good. And you get through the day. You repeat the same damn thing the next day, and the next. You put that fake smile on and show that fucker you're good!"

"Okay, Dad, I will," were Maggie's mumbled words. She finally fell into a deep sleep while Zip comforted and stroked her hair.

*Quite the day,* Zip thought. Between listening to Biggs and Maggie he understood why he was exhausted. Obviously, he was grateful he could be present for his daughter, but seeing Biggs trust him enough to share what he and Jessica had endured deepened his friendship with Biggs. After so much self-doubt and loathing he felt honored that someone would trust him and appreciate his counseling.

A few nights later, around 10:00 p.m., Zip sat peacefully at his kitchen counter watching drone footage of the layout at Sacramento Country Club on his laptop. Maggie had long gone to bed, thankfully. She had had a rough week but held her promise to stand tall at school. He carefully moved his mouse so the drone on his computer screen would provide every detail of each hole at this particular golf course. He diligently scribbled notes and looked for advantages on the layout as Sac CC was the golf course where he and Biggs chose to play a qualifier for the US Open.

Sacramento wasn't far from where they lived, so they figured they could have an advantage by not having to travel too far. A cold Red Stripe sat next to him. Beads of condensation dripped down the side of the bottle. Zip lit a scented candle, eucalyptus, hoping that its aroma could help clear his mind and build on the creativity he anticipated he'd need to loop Biggs through such an important round. Sac CC's layout wasn't long. But it was extremely penal with thick nasty roughs bordering very narrow fairways.

"This place reminds me of EV." He smiled, as he took a sip of his beer. "We could have a shot here."

He continued to guide his mouse through each and every nook and cranny of the course. He paused the mouse over areas where he could mark the yardages and evaluate specific trees and penalty areas. The notepad next to his laptop was filling up fast. Zip was feeling excited as he sat in the quiet of the night. A small lamp on the counter and the screen from the laptop provided the only light. He was in a zone that only a caddy would know when suddenly there was a knock at the front door. Zip was fairly antisocial and at this time of night he knew any knock at the door couldn't be good.

"It's fucking 10:30 p.m., who the hell?" he grumbled, as he checked the clock on his microwave.

"Hi, sir. I apologize if I'm bothering you, but is Maggie home? I know it's late but I *have* to talk to her," Jake stammered when Zip opened the front door.

"Kind of late, isn't it, pal? Didn't your mom teach you any manners?" Zip replied, clearly trying to throw a dig into Jake. "She's here, in her room. How about texting her?"

"Sir, please. I know you're not fond of me."

"Fond?!" Zip cracked. "You're a punk! You hurt my daughter and when you hurt her, you hurt me. I'd say fond is an understatement, to say the least!"

"Yes, I know, sir, I know. I wholeheartedly apologize. I'm confused. I wasn't thinking clearly," Jake whined.

"Look, kid, and my name is John so enough with the 'sir' bullshit. You guys are young. You both have no idea what you're doing. This won't be the first time you have a relationship go south. Just deal with it. The emotions, all of it. It's part of growing up. The sun will rise tomorrow. Move on with your life."

Jake just stood on the porch, head down. He realized he wasn't getting in.

"Si . . . I mean John, could you please let me speak to her? I bought prom tickets and . . ."

"Prom! Listen, Jake, she's moved on. I hope mommy didn't waste too much money on those tickets. Find someone else to take. You've got time. You're a nice looking kid. I'm sure there's someone that will go with you, but it ain't going to be Maggie!"

Zip stepped out onto the porch and closed the door behind him. He knew Maggie wasn't completely over the breakup. He definitely did not want her to hear them conversing as she might come out of her room and cave in to Jake and his desperate prom offer.

"It's best if you go, bud," Zip sternly ordered.

"But si . . . sorry, I mean John, if you'd just let me spea—"

"Get the fuck out of here, dude!" Zip interrupted. "I'm super busy and don't have time for this shit. She's over you, dude. Hit the bricks," he barked.

Jake turned around to walk back down the path. Halfway to the front gate at the end of the yard he turned and yelled, "MAGGIE!"

"Goddamnit! Get the fuck out of here, you little shit, before I lodge a 9 iron up your ass!" Zip yelled.

He charged towards Jake, who proceeded to now run towards his truck. As he opened his truck's door, he turned to Zip and with a girlish shriek, tears in his eyes, cried out, "You never liked me. I knew it. I'm going to get her back, I swear!"

"Oh, don't swear, Jakey," Zip said mockingly, imitating the name he was sure Jake's mother often called her son. "Your mommy might get mad. And one more thing, Jakey . . . THANK YOU FOR HAVING ME!"

Zip erupted in laughter as Jake peeled away in his truck, screeching his tires like a drag racer. Maggie was at the front door when Zip came back in.

"Dad, was that who I think it was?"

"Yes, honey. I'm so proud of you. Go back to bed."

"Night, Dad. And thanks."

"You got it, kiddo," he told her softly.

Maggie went off to her room and Zip returned to his laptop. His beer was now warm which only contributed to his disdain for Jake. Why he was even engaging in such immature behavior with a punk like Jake baffled him. Was he being too harsh with the kid? Was it the Red Stripes and yellowbirds that made him sink to such levels? Probably. But for whatever reason he wasn't going to let up on a kid who hurt Maggie, even if it meant stooping to Jake's level. And to elevate the scorn he felt towards Jake, now, after all that, his beer was warm. He dumped it out, grabbed a fresh one, and dug back into his course study. It was nearly 4:00 a.m. before Zip closed the laptop for the night. He had poured over every inch of Sacramento Country Club. He knew this was as much a chance for redemption for him as it was for Biggs. He was going to be as prepared as one could possibly be. He owed that to Maggie, to Biggs, and, as importantly, to himself.

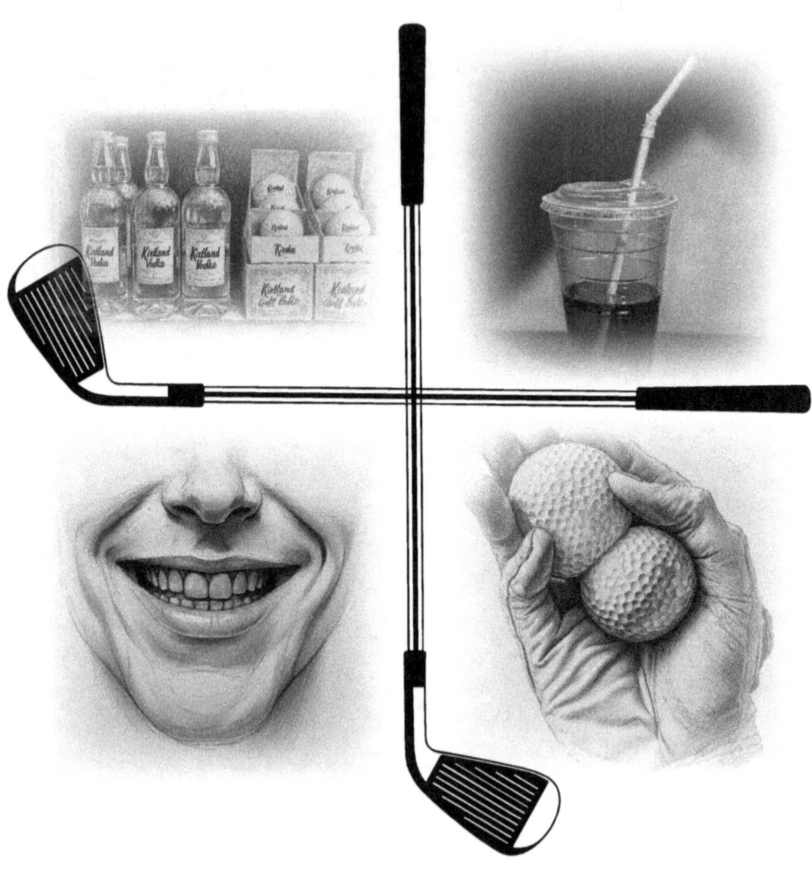

## HOLE #13

"Boys, I'm bringing a guest today," Zip announced, as as he and Biggs walked onto the practice screen at Eagle Vista.

The other guys in the group had been preoccupied with their warm-ups. Their heads were down, practicing putts of various distances. But when they heard Zip, they all peeked up in unison like a bunch of chickens that simultaneously sensed there was a fox in the chicken coop.

"Christ, where you been, Zip?" growled LH. "Word is you're going big time. Trying to take Biggs to the US Open? Good luck with that," he continued, in his antagonistic surliness.

"Pay no attention to him," Zip said to Biggs. "He's a curmudgeon. We call him LH because he's a short little man and that tiny mustache and comb over . . . well, he's the spitting image of Hitler. So 'Little Hitler' morphed into LH for short. It's just easier to say and, believe it or not, he's clueless to what LH stands for. He updates everyone's handicaps and scores on a home computer. He's an awful player that gives you unsolicited swing tips and tells you how to play certain shots. Whatever you do, do not listen to him."

"Got it." Biggs laughed.

"Hey, nice to meet you, my name is Paul." He reached out to shake Biggs' hand. "Heard you're a stick. Trying to make the US Open? That's amazing."

Paul was a genuinely nice dude. He was the artist of a group that consisted of roughly twenty guys who regularly golfed together. They were from all walks of life and ability and liked to gamble a few dollars when they played. They were a band of brothers that never called each other by their real names. Only the nicknames they'd been given. They were a close-knit group that shared one common skill. It wasn't playing golf. It was drinking booze. Each weekend these guys would show up at Eagle Vista intent on three things— getting drunk, getting away from spouses, and possibly shooting a good score— in exactly that order. If the latter happened, it was simply a bonus. But more often than not, it didn't. Having thick skin was a requirement as the more you didn't like your nickname, the more you'd be stuck with it.

"Yeah, we're going to give it a run," Biggs replied to Paul. "Zip here has me in training."

"Hey, Pablo," Zip interrupted. "Jesus, dude, did your cat sleep on your sweatshirt? And, of course, you don't have a belt to tuck that tattered shirt that's hanging out into those paint-splattered shorts? This is a country club not an art studio!"

Paul was every bit an artist. In fact, the boys labeled him Pablo because it was similar to Paul and linked to his favorite artist, Picasso. Pablo's brain wasn't wired to care about his clothing. If his socks matched, that was a bonus. When it rained, he'd wear the only waterproof shoes he owned that were not golf shoes of course. The shoes he wore were, of course, neither made for golf or waterproof. They were these low rise, faux leather walking loafers that were too big and he practically came out of when he swung. The group determined they resembled prison slippers and when it was wet out, he'd slide around like an ice skater. It was only when someone gave him an old pair of golf shoes did he stop slipping everywhere. He had plenty of money to buy proper golf stuff. He just didn't care. He was always happy. Always smiling. Zip thought of Pablo like a little brother and loved razzing him.

"Give us a smile, Pablo," Zip demanded. "We want to see if it's a cabernet or sauvignon blanc day? Welp, there it is . . . today's teeth have a nice red hue to them. Must be a cab day. You got your plastic cup with the straw? Classy."

"Right here," Pablo said, as he pulled a huge, clear plastic cup full to the top with red wine from his golf cart. He loved to drink red wine from a clear plastic cup with a lid and straw that protected him from spilling onto a black sweatshirt infested with cat hair that he'd wear in sweltering heat. And if said heat had warmed up his cup 'o wine, so be it. He was beautiful in that he simply didn't care about his appearance or what anyone thought.

"You kiss your wife with that mouth?" Biggs joked, feeling comfortable enough to join the ribbing. "Between the cabernet and the Copenhagen your teeth look like you bit your tongue chewing ants. Make sure you run a toothbrush across those things before you go home."

"You're going to fit right in with this group, Biggs." Pablo laughed. "And, yes, I'll make sure I do that before I see her."

Pete was next to approach and introduce himself. Pete was known as "the Commish" because he was a founding member of the group and generally made the tee times for them to play. He also liked to govern over various controversies and decisions that periodically arose. And with a group of knuckleheads that size, there were many. The Commish would be at his computer at 6:00 a.m. most days locking in tee times for the group. He took his position seriously. It gave him self-worth. It was a simple task that anyone could easily do, but the Commish did it well and never hesitated to tell the group they should be more grateful for his efforts. He thrived on the attention. Therefore, the group patronized him by giving him the Commish moniker. Simply put, he didn't hate it.  Zip considered him a diva.

Pete also loved to talk about himself. In fact, most of the boys in the group did. Listening was a rarity. Talking about yourself wasn't. They didn't actually listen to "what" someone was saying. Instead, they'd listen to "when" that someone would end their sentence, or stop talking, and then they'd immediately pounce on that silence to start talking about themselves.

Someone might say, "My wife was just diagnosed with cancer . . ." only to immediately be interrupted by another guy saying, "Oh, I had the worst indigestion last night."

The Commish, in all his diva-ness, was the king of self-indulgence. Starting conversations with him was like going down a rabbit hole. Zip learned this the hard way. All too often in the past Zip would belly up next to Pete at the bar and simply ask one question about

Pete's health or his golf game and come to realize, there'd go a half hour to 45 minutes of Pete's pomposity.

"Your name is Biggs? Nice to meet you. I'm Pete. They call me the Commish. I hear you're pretty good? Played on the Korn Ferry tour?"

"Pretty good?!" LH sarcastically barked. "He's a plus four. Shot a 65 the other day and before that broke the course record."

"Told you he'd know your shit," Zip laughed. I guarantee he's been tracking your rounds."

"I was on Korn Ferry a few years back. Enjoyed the experience," Biggs humbly said to Pete.

"Yeah, I know what it's like to play at a high level. I played pro pro baseball," bragged Pete.

"Easy, Pedro, two months riding a Greyhound in A ball isn't exactly the pro baseball experience one might think of," cracked Zip.

"If it wasn't for a bad back, Ida made the big leagues," Pete replied, defending himself.

"Funny, last week it was your knee," Zip teased, remembering the rabbit hole he went down at the bar last week after asking Pete about his baseball career.

"Anyway," Pete continued, trying his best to ignore Zip, "I wish you the best." Pete shot Zip an annoyed look. He knew he'd been outed which was frustrating because he prized new fresh ears that hadn't yet tasted his bullshit.

"Hey, are we going to play or bullshit?" grumbled LH. "I don't think Biggs should be in our bet. He's too good."

"That's fine," Zip said. "We all know you'd rather pay income taxes than lose $10. We're just out here to work on some things. I can't have my player even remotely concentrating on your ugly game anyway," he laughed. "And, please, do not give him any of your swing tips. He has rabbit ears, as it is, and I can't have you telling him he's all arms or not turning. His swing is a Rembrandt and yours is paint by numbers, so leave him be."

Only Pablo laughed loudly at Zip's comment because the others assumed Rembrandt was a YouTube golf instructor.

THWAAK! LH shanked an ugly grounder off the first tee that rolled out about 30 yards. He immediately grabbed his left shoulder and started rotating it as if he was injured.

"Goddammit that hurt," he moaned.

"That's interesting because you shanked a similar

shot the other day and grabbed your right shoulder. You must be falling apart," Zip quipped.

"Take a hike," LH snarled. Such a biting comeback was about as good as LH could muster.

The Commish stepped up and with an athletic baseball swing smashed a nice line drive that found the fairway.

"Commish, you look good today," yelled Hondo.

Hondo was another regular in the group who was standing just off the 1st tee waiting his turn. His first name was Tom. Last name was Henderson. But no one called him by either. It was purely Hondo.

"New pants?" Hondo asked the Commish.

"Yep, Costco, $14," he responded.

"I loves me some Costco," Hondo chimed in. "The Kirkland balls and wedges are conveniently right next to the vodka. I'm in and out. But not before some free samples and a hot dog for the road."

"That's called target marketing, by the way. Costco sees you guys comin' from a mile away. They strategically put the golf equipment next to the vodka for a reason. They know the real reason you go . . . and it ain't for the golf stuff," heckled Zip.

"Who's the Costco lover?" Biggs asked.

"That's Hondo," Zip replied. "He's originally from Boston. Steer clear cuz he loves his cocktails and by day's end he'll convince you to somehow buy him one, or three. He's a true professional . . . drinker, that is. Most days he strolls down from the parking lot to the 1st tee by 7:00 a.m. and doesn't stumble back up until around 9:00 p.m., after the bar closes. With no less than 20-30 cocktails in him.

"You'd think he'd be crushed. But like clockwork, he's right back here again the following morning. See that towel he tucks into the back of his shorts? He wears it because he thinks he looks like a QB. He worships Tom Brady. Stole it from the bathroom of a hotel where we stayed on a golf trip. Never mind that it's black with gold embroidered letters that say Peppermill Casino and looks ridiculous. He wears it religiously. He's a beaut."

"Where's your clubs, Zip?" Pablo asked, as he loosened up waving his driver back and forth.

"I'm just going to caddy today. I've got some work to do with my player."

"How does the US Open work? Like, don't you need to be on the PGA tour?" Pablo curiously asked.

"Not necessarily," LH interrupted. "You just need to have a .04 cap and then play well in a local qualifier, then again at a 36-hole final qualifier. There's a local qualifier near here in Sacramento in a few weeks. Then the final is at Harding Park," he added.

"Your knowledge never ceases to amaze me, LH," Zip said. "We might think about switching your nickname to Rain Man. It would definitely be fitting. Yeah, if I can get my guy through the Sac tourney, I feel great about Harding. I know that place like the back of my hand," he continued.

"Geez, I really hope you guys can do it," Pablo said. Pablo was next to hit. He unleashed a huge drive and immediately screamed, "Oh, shit!" Not only did the golf ball take off, but his driver slipped out of his hands and helicoptered about 30 to 40 yards from the tee.

"Good lord!" Zip yelled. "How many times have I told you to get your clubs re-gripped?! They're like holding icicles."

"I know, I know." Pablo laughed sheepishly. "I'll do it, I promise," he said, though Pablo had absolutely no intention of ever following through with it.

"Yeah, right! Your brain isn't wired to do that. Look at your socks, one's brown and one's gray!" Zip remarked.

Biggs was next and stepped up to the tee. By this time most of the other players from the practice green and bar patrons had surrounded the 1st tee. Word had spread around EV about the skillset Biggs possessed and how one of their fellow members was trying for the US Open. With Zip on his bag, no less. Biggs ripped a beautiful high fade that felt like it dangled in the air a full minute before falling to the middle of the fairway. There was tons of commotion, whispering, and mumbling going on around the tee. Biggs however, heard nothing. As he walked off the tee, he wondered if Zip's training methods were actually working.

"Nice!" Zip said. "Look, today we're just playing tee to green golf. They can move the pins but they can't move the center of the green. Just try to block out all the BS. These guys aren't too bad but there's a few guys that chatter nonstop. The type of guys that constantly brag about how they bought Apple stock before anyone. Of course, they bought Nvidia before it took off. Know everything about Bitcoin. They talk about wineries like they are all sommeliers. God help us if they're taking an upcoming trip somewhere because you'll get every detail. Not today. Today we play our game. No distractions."

"Got it," Biggs simply replied.

"If anyone brings up LIV golf, they're dead," warned Zip. "And if I see one of you doing that two finger aim point bullshit or spreading your feet to judge the slope or breaks on the greens I'm going to wrap a putter around your head!"

The Commish made birdie on the very first hole. Being quite proud of himself, during the 25-yard walk between the first and second tee, he proceeded to voice every detail of how he played the hole. He even pulled out his 8 iron to show the group the mark the ball left on his club face where he struck his second shot. Zip was less than thrilled.

"That's what we call NBC," he whispered to Biggs, as the Commish continued detailing his putt.

"NBC?" Biggs queried.

"No Body Cares."

When they reached the second hole, the Commish was due to hit first as was custom after making birdie.

"Birdie shots!" yelled a giddy LH.  "I've got Fireball." LH reached into his bag and pulled out an eight pack of airline size bottles of Firebird, all neatly packaged in rows of four, wrapped in plastic.

"Love one," the Commish said.

"Me too," chimed Pablo. "Biggs, are you down?"

"Hell, no!" Zip blurted out. "It's 8:00 friggin' a.m. in the morning, my player isn't slamming Fireball!"

"To each his own," Pablo replied, as the other three toasted the Commish's achievement.

"No sense waiting for these fools, go ahead and hit," Zip told Biggs, who obliged by hammering a rocket of a drive straight down the middle.

The Commish followed and promptly shanked a high cutting slice well over a group of tall trees that protected a row of homes halfway down the fairway.

"That's gone," Zip informed the group. "You want to reload? I'm sure that birdie shot didn't help," he chuckled.

"I don't know. I thought I heard it hit something," the Commish protested.

"Yeah, maybe you heard it hit a car parked in the driveway in front of one of those houses!" Pablo said sarcastically.

As they walked down the fairway the Commish blazed past them in his cart to go find his ball that the rest of the group already knew was out.

"Here we go, watch this," Zip told Biggs.

"What's going on?" Biggs asked.

"Oh, he'll find it, trust me," Zip explained. "He actually carries a few balls with yellow tree marks on them so when he hits one OB like he just did he'll pretend it hit a tree and stayed in. Watch, he'll tell you."

"Quite the group here." Biggs smirked.

They kept their heads down as they walked towards Biggs' ball, purposely not wanting to pay attention to the shenanigans that were about to happen. After the Commish drove around the area where his ball clearly left the yard, he turned and drove over towards them.

"I guess you were right," he said. "It must've gone out. I could have sworn I heard something."

Pablo was walking up the fairway in that same general area and the Commish motioned to him.

"Hey, Pablo, since you're walking that way, do you mind taking a quick look for my ball?"

"Oh, this is rich," Zip muttered quietly to Biggs.

"What the F. . ?" Biggs asked curiously.

"Here's what he'll do, I've seen this before. He drives up there before anyone can see anything and he'll toss one of his balls with the yellow tree marks near the out of bounds. Then he pretends he can't find his ball, so he pulls away but will ask someone else to look. It's a classic maneuver."

Just then, like clockwork, Pablo, who was about 30 yards further down the fairway than where Zip had watched the Commish's ball sail over a rooftop, yelled out, "Hey, Pete, you playing a Kirkland?"

"Oh, shit! Yes!" the Commish exclaimed, trying to act completely surprised.

"Pablo coulda' asked if he hit a Pinnacle Gold and the Commish would've said yes!" Zip scoffed.

Biggs stepped up and hit a nice draw that settled 10 feet from the pin.

"Attaboy. Try not to be distracted by all the shenanigans. Think of Rusty." Zip giggled.

They got up to his ball and began to assess the line and the break.

"What do you think?" Biggs asked Zip.

"The hole is a friggin' salad bowl. Don't overthink it."

Biggs struck his putt and it rolled perfectly to the hole. But just as it was about to go in it hit a small indentation on the green where someone earlier had not sufficiently fixed their ball mark causing the ball to stop a few inches from the hole.

"Typical EV," Zip commented. "People just don't fix their ball marks. Stay clear of the bunkers, too, because you'll surely end up in a big ole footprint. People drive me nuts. But, hey, like I always say, tap in par, take 'em all day. There's nothing worse than having a 5-footer left for par. Was it Trevino that said two things that won't last long are dogs chasing cars and pros chasing pars?"

"Tap in par, take 'em all day?" Biggs repeated. "I like that one."

On the next tee, the Commish approached the group with his ball in his hand. "Hey, look at this," he announced. "You can actually see the yellow mark where it hit the tree."

Biggs glanced over to Zip, who was discreetly shaking his head. "Let's keep it moving boys. We've got some work to do today," Zip said, with a smile.

Right before Pablo was about to tee off on the next hole, a long par 5, they saw a couple walking their dog along the cart path that lined the left side of the fairway.

"You gotta be kidding me," LH said, in disgust. "Hey, this is a golf course not a fucking park!" he screamed.

The couple looked up at the golfers. They were surprised and completely oblivious to the fact that their Saturday morning stroll that provided their dog his daily constitution was in fact a golf course. But by this time the dog was fully focused on his task at hand as he squatted on the finely cut grass near a tree.

"Jesus, you're joking, right!?" LH yelled.

The group, not wanting to maim the couple or their precious Fido with an errant shot, impatiently waited for the mutt to finish his business. They must've figured, since it was a large green open space, they were entitled to use it as they pleased. LH yelled at them to clear out, but one of the dog's owners yelled back that it was okay to hit into them because they could "see" the players and therefore weren't in any danger zone. Little did they know that, other than Biggs, these guys generally had no idea where their ball was headed once they hit it and could easily put a ball on top of them. The couple just smiled and waved to the group as one of them bent over to baggy Fido's freshly laid delivery while everyone waited.

"People, man." A frustrated Zip shook his head. "I'd almost tell you to send them a message pitch but let's just let them clear out and concentrate on what we're doing."

Biggs played fabulously as the group continued their round. He actually enjoyed the banter from the other players and found their unique personalities to be a refreshing contrast to the dead serious golf geeks he used to play with. Word had gotten around Eagle Vista that Zip and this new stick were out on the course preparing for a run at the US Open. As in any club, real pros playing their course was a novelty. However, gossip was not. So, as the boys played hole after hole, more and more people that had heard the scoop started to come watch. The 9th hole finished near the clubhouse. By that point nearly 75 to 100 people were out on the deck adjacent to the bar overlooking the 9th green and 10th tee box. A thick Eagle Vista gallery had assembled, eager to watch this new pro. There was a hum of chatter and whispers as folks talked about what they'd heard about Biggs.

On the 10th tee, Biggs turned to Zip. "What do you think? Is this getting weird?" he asked, as the crowd moved from the deck and surrounded the tee.

"No, this is perfect," Zip replied. "Give the folks a show. I know one thing, poor LH and the Commish are going to shit down both legs trying to hit in front of all these folks. We have 9 holes left. Two of them are par 5s so those are easy birdies. I'll tell you what. Maggie has every episode of *The Bachelor* recorded. For every birdie you make, you won't have to watch an episode. For every par, you're going to watch a full episode all the way to the rose ceremony. And don't even think about making worse than par cuz I've got *90 Day Fiancé* cued up if you do."

Zip blurted out these instructions loudly enough for everyone to hear. From the laughter that followed, it was apparent the gallery loved the challenge as well.

"Bro, are you serious? *The Bachelor?* That show sucks! I'd rather scratch my eyes out," Biggs pleaded.

"Well, you better make some birdies then," Pablo snarked, and spat red- colored Copenhagen juice, a consequence of his nasty chew with wine mix, onto the grass.

"Damn, Pablo!" Zip bemoaned. "I've heard dentists have high suicide rates, but those teeth would send any of them off the Golden Gate Bridge."

Biggs played flawlessly as he started the back 9. He birdied the par 4 10th and 11th. He stuck a wedge on the par 3 12th to a foot. Then easily birdied the par 5 13th. The crowd followed every shot. They yelled words of support and cheered after each putt he sank. On the 14th hole Biggs addressed a 15-foot curler for birdie.

"I've heard there's lots of tears at the rose ceremony," Zip interrupted, trying to throw some shade towards his players' momentum. "Or is tonight a home visit? Those are always riveting. Maybe we should slam a beer every time we hear 'I could definitely see myself falling in love with you.'"

"It's going to break to the left," LH blurted out, trying to insert himself into the situation.

"Wait, wait, wait," Zip intervened. "Do not listen to him. Remember what I said?"

Biggs putted the ball exactly opposite of LH's advice and sunk it for his 5th straight birdie.

"Uh-oh, the course record you set a few weeks ago could be in jeopardy," the Commish chimed in. "I remember setting the season home run record in college and single game record the next . . ."

"Hold it! Hold it! No, sir, no way!" Zip said, as he again stepped in to cut off the Commish. "My player's in a zone. We're not doing that," he bluntly told him.

The small gallery was creating a ruckus as they followed this display of golf. Most of them carried cocktails as they walked and cheered. The other players in the group were clearly affected, not to mention scared shitless, at being forced to hit shots in front of such a gathering. Biggs was unfazed. It was apparent that he was unbothered by the fact that folks wielding cocktails were lingering no less than 10 yards from him before he'd hit a shot. They also paid little attention to golf etiquette regarding noise. Just prior to his approach shot on the par 4 15th, Zip raised his arms as if to ask the crowd to finally be quiet. They obliged, and as Zip anticipated, the quiet unnerved Biggs a bit and he uncharacteristically hit a poor shot that landed in a greenside bunker. He was still able to get up and down for a par. But his concentration, or lack thereof, cost him a chance at another birdie.

"Oh, Maggie's gonna be pumped! She's got someone to watch her shows with," gloated Zip. "That's one episode right there."

The 16th was a par 5 and Biggs again easily made birdie. The crowd was back to their normal noise level. Zip hadn't asked them to quiet down for a while. On the 17th hole, a long par 3, Zip again raised his arms and asked for silence. Biggs hit a decent fade that landed 30 feet or so from the pin. A decent shot, but clearly not his best.

"Looks like we need to get back into the lab a bit," Zip said.

"Ugh!" Biggs yelled out, after his ball landed so far from the pin. "I can make that putt though." However, he just barely missed the putt as the ball came to a stop a few inches from the hole.

"Tap in par, take them all day," Biggs proclaimed. "Crap, that's two shows now. Guess I'm making popcorn," he laughed loudly.

Biggs went on to birdie 18 with a fabulous second shot that nuzzled four feet from the hole and easily sank the putt.

"What time should I be over?" he asked Zip.

"Let me check with Maggie. I'll see when she's finished with her homework. She'll be excited."

Biggs hadn't broken his own course record. The crowd dispersed and many went back into the bar that was now buzzing with what they'd all witnessed. A few patrons approached Biggs to wish him luck.

"Make sure you post your score!" LH snarled at Biggs.

They all shook hands and walked off the 18th green. Zip turned to Biggs,

"Maybe they'll let us play music in the qualifiers but I doubt it," he joked. "Don't worry, you're making great progress. I'll see you around 8:00 p.m."

Zip stopped at the club bar after the round. He hadn't been in such a good mood in quite a while. Although there was much work to do, Biggs was responding to his methods which gave him a sense of purpose that felt good. Feeling good meant celebrating. And the only way an alcoholic such as himself knew to celebrate was beers at the bar. Most of the members had filed back into the bar and he longed to satisfy another alcoholic disorder which was to get his ego stroked, a sensation he also hadn't felt in a long time. The cocktail-toting patrons that had just witnessed how good a player Biggs was were more than willing to blindly assume that Zip's instructions had anything to do with it. After a few beers and inane chit-chat from the many wannabe Jim Nances that approached him to discuss the upcoming qualifiers, which he relished, his phone pinged that familiar sound.

*Birds are in,* was the simple text from JD.
*Fabulous, perfect timing. How many?*
*I'll be there in 10,* Zip immediately and joyfully replied.
*Plenty, get over here,* JD answered.

Zip jumped in his cart and eagerly beelined towards JD's house. After such a great day on the course nothing seemed better than an evening of continued beers and pill consumption. He raced down the sidewalk towards an ATM to get the required funds for JD, ignoring the commute traffic on the busy street next to him and completely disregarding any concern for law enforcement. He had the necessary players for tonight's party and in his mind it was game on.

"I can't hang long, JD. I've got someone coming over," were the hasty words he blurted out, as he greeted

JD and maneuvered through the maze of a hoarder's paradise.

JD was dressed in a goose down jacket that was torn around the shoulder, ski beanie, baggy sweatpants, and combat boots.

"Dude it's almost 90 degrees out! You look like you're going skiing!" Zip said.

"I know, I know, I can't get warm. I've tried hot soup. Layers of clothing. I'm not feeling well," JD answered, as he let out a deep chest cough.

"How many birds you doing a day, man? Maybe that has something to do with it. You sound like you have pneumonia."

"Actually, I've cut way back. Haven't done *any*. I need the money. I'm definitely dope sick," JD replied, coughing even more.

"Oh, shit. That's too bad. Okay, well I'll take 50 if you've got them?" Zip said, ignoring any sympathy towards JD. The lack of empathy isn't uncommon for drug addicted alcoholics. When the bender's in full force, there isn't time for sympathy.

He handed his friend a wad of cash, jumped back in the cart, and sped downhill towards his house.

"Maggie?! We're going to have company, hun. Someone's finally going to watch *The Bachelor* with you!" he yelled, as he entered through the garage.

"Seriously?" a surprised Maggie answered. "Who is it?"

"My golf buddy. He loves the show."

"Awesome, Dad. Can we make popcorn?"

"Without a doubt, hun. Crappy television and empty carbs sound like a great evening to me."

Biggs arrived about a half hour later, a six pack of Red Stripes in tow.

"Heard you liked these. I thought about buying a case cuz that's the only way I'll get through the night. But I told Jess I wouldn't be out late."

"I've got plenty, trust me," Zip said, with a smile.

After the first episode finished, Zip quietly snuck back down the hallway into his room, leaving Biggs and Maggie in the living room.

"Maggie, I've heard good things about you"—Biggs smiled—"but being a fan of this crap knocks you down a bit."

"It's good old dumb trash, I know," she answered. "But dumb trash is what I need right now. This dude I was dating won't stop badgering me to get back together with him. In fact, he's getting a little psycho."

"He *should* regret it. Look at you. You're a great kid. To hell with him," Biggs counseled.

"Sounds like you've been talking to my dad," Maggie joked.

"Where's the bathroom?" Biggs asked her.

"Down the hall on your left."

Biggs walked down a dark hallway and mistakenly went into Zip's room. Zip was startled. He was standing next to his dresser holding a prescription bottle and a handful of pills in one hand, a Red Stripe in the other.

"You sick, dude?" Biggs asked. "What are those?"

"Oh, these are little happy pills. Want one?" Zip stammered. He was clearly inebriated by this point. Not even trying to hide anything.

"Happy pills? Painkillers? You fucking kidding me?!" Biggs bellowed.

"Hey, chill, I'm just partying."

"Look I've seen firsthand what that shit does to people. I fucking need you, Zip! This was YOUR fucking idea! I've already got one person I love that can't get out of bed, so don't be the second person I desperately need going south on me. PLEASE!"

Biggs reached out to swipe the script bottle from Zip's hand and Zip blocked his grasp protecting his stash as if it were a bar of gold.

"Look if you're going to be a fucking junkie, then we're through. Fuck this whole thing!" Biggs yelled.

"Oh, come on!" Zip fired back.

Biggs was already briskly walking out the front door towards his car. Before getting in he turned back towards Zip. "I fucking believe in you, Zip! Don't fucking do this to me!" He was devastated by what he'd witnessed. He jumped in his car and peeled away.

"Dad, what's going on? Why did Biggs leave? We have another show," Maggie asked, after hearing all the commotion.

"Don't worry about it, Maggie," Zip muttered.

He stood on his front porch. Hands on his hips. A little bit in shock as he watched Biggs pull away.

"Fuck," was all he could muster under his breath.

That next morning, or basically early afternoon, came a huge bang. It wasn't from any actual noise. It came from the pounding in Zip's head. He checked his phone.

*Dad, I tried waking you like three times. Thought you were dead. LOL. I got a ride*, Maggie wrote.

The next text was from Biggs. *Zip, barely slept. I'm at the range. Dude, please, please don't let me down. I'll let this slide, won't mention it. Just need you to promise me you'll stop that bullshit. Please, Zip.*

Zip sat on the edge of his bed in his room darkened by his curtains that blocked a beautiful sunny day. He knew he couldn't blow this opportunity like he'd done many times before with various situations. His addiction was at a tipping point and he knew something needed to be done.

14

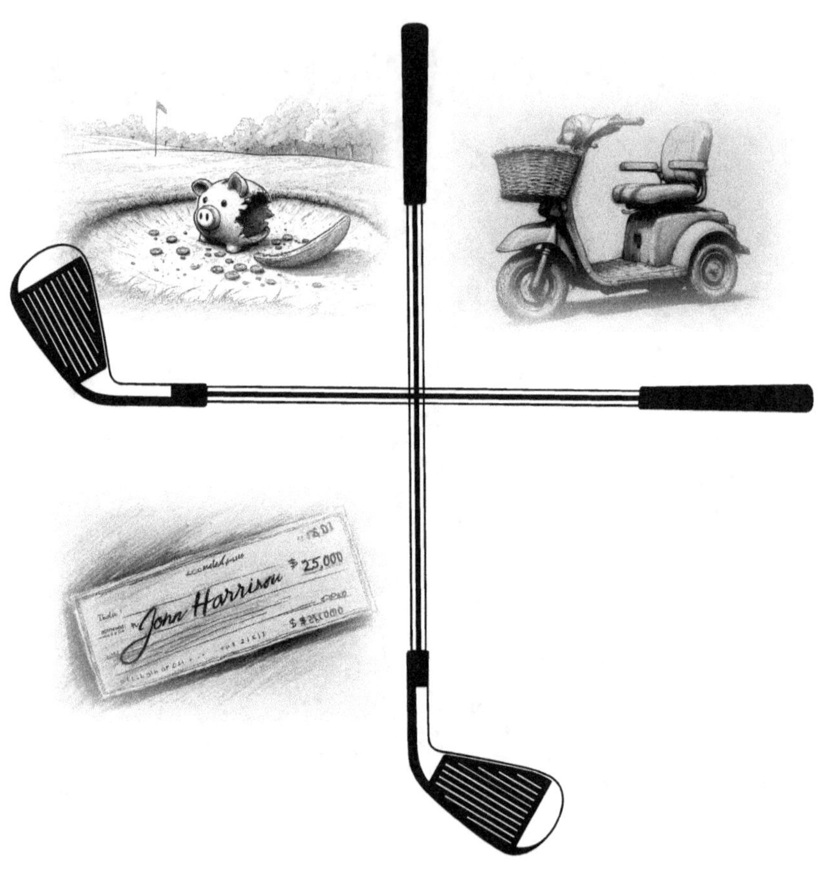

## HOLE #14

He reached for his phone. Knew there was one person to call. Definitely not JD. Zip had a childhood friend named Craig. They grew up on the same street. And because everyone had a nickname in Zip's life, they paid tribute to that fact by calling each other appropriately, "Street." Zip and Street had known each other for some 45 years. They met the summer prior to high school when they'd been hired to rip shingles off the roof of a house. Now Zip considered himself a pretty strong dude, but he kept looking at this other kid that seemed to relentlessly rip twice as many shingles off as Zip could. Zip even told the kid to slow down a bit as they were being paid by the hour. Street and Zip bonded on that rooftop over the next few weeks.

There's no blueprint for how lifelong friendships are made but effort is a huge factor and Street gave every bit of effort possible when it came to any type of work. He was genuine and loyal. Traits Zip shared. Their bond grew easily. They'd been through many of life's curveballs together. They hid nothing from each other. Street knew of Zip's struggles. Fifteen years ago, Street wasn't delivered a curveball, in fact, he was dealt a Nolan Ryan fastball. A 12-round fight with Mike Tyson. He was jogging on a treadmill when he felt a lightning bolt type of pain shoot up his left leg. His back had been bothering him. His muscles were acting erratic and spastic.

After many months and many tests trying to discover why he was suffering, Street was finally diagnosed with multiple sclerosis. The next fifteen years was one punch after another ostensibly getting pummeled by this unforgiving disease as his once incredibly strong body withered away. Street was once an athlete. He played offensive line in high school. He blocked for Zip, who was a running back. He was a beast in the weight room. He could deadlift 450 lbs. and squat 400 lbs. and that was in high school! He consistently exercised. He wasn't a great athlete, but he also loved playing basketball and golf.

As an adult he built a lucrative real estate business and became extremely wealthy. To watch this once pillar of strength diminish into a figure that was now bound to a wheelchair was beyond heartbreaking. Street tried every treatment, every medication. There was nothing to stop the progression of his MS. Street's brain, however, worked perfectly which for him was almost cruel because he was totally cognizant while he watched his body debilitate. He and Zip shared hours of conversations. How could such an advanced medical society not find a cure? They hypothesized that perhaps MS didn't affect enough people so that the powers that be would throw every resource possible into finding a way to stop the progression.

Street's inordinate wealth mattered little in his battle to stop MS's indifference between the *haves* and *have-nots*. Perhaps, in the future, that time will come. Unfortunately, not soon enough for Street. Zip counseled Street when he was down, which was often. But Street was the toughest SOB Zip knew and always displayed a good attitude to others. But Street got real with Zip and Zip got real with Street.

Often Street told Zip that today was the day. That he'd wished he had a 44 caliber because he couldn't take it anymore. He had a girlfriend that was a saint and helped him immensely. Zip called her Saint Anna. Saint Anna came into Street's life not long after his wife asked for a divorce which was coldly a few months after his diagnosis. His symptoms hadn't begun to shred his body yet, but his wife knew the future and didn't have the stones to deal with it. But Anna entered fearlessly and sacrificed so much of her life to care for this man.

"I'm in trouble," Zip said, as Street answered his phone. "I got to get off this junk."

"*You're* in trouble?" Street barked sarcastically. "I went to take a piss at 3:00 a.m., fell off my scooter, and lodged myself between the toilet and the bathroom wall. Anna couldn't lift me. Had to call the fire department just to come lift me back into bed. You ever had five firemen AND women pick you up stark naked cuz you can't get your ass off the floor!?"

"Oh, no. Sorry, brother. But how 'bout the poor firemen? I doubt when they were training to be first responders they knew that might include picking up a crippled, hairy, naked guy off the bathroom floor," Zip joked.

Both of them chuckled. Of course, Street's predicament was far from being considered funny, in fact quite the opposite. But these two lifelong friends struggled together. Being open and accepting of their diseases with each other was therapy. Street had been dealt an awful hand. Obviously much worse than Zip's. But since neither of them could rely on any scientific advancements to help, they proved that laughter was indeed the best medicine.

"I've been telling you for a long time now you're going to face a day of reckoning," Street bluntly told his friend.

"I know. I'm sitting on an opportunity to do something great with a player I've taken under my tutelage, so to speak," Zip replied.

"Easy with the 'tutelage,' Berkeley. Remember, I went to junior college," Street joked. "What kind of hairbrained opportunity are you talking about? Does he know you're a drunk that sleeps till noon? Hold on a second, I have another call."

After about a minute, Street returned.

"Jesus, I'm telling you, Zip, people. That was Jack. Going on and on about how he's depressed and how *his* life is *so* difficult. Something about his kids driving him nuts and his air conditioning not working. Do you know how good able people have it? I'd do anything for his problems. I'd give up everything I have, every dime. I'd live under a fucking bridge if I could have my health!"

Street's humorous tone had shifted. Now he was simply agitated. "So, what's your problem? You're going to fuck up another opportunity because you're an idiot that drinks too much and loves hanging out with that, speaking of living under bridges, fucking troll of a human being JD we knew in high school? Get it together! You have ZERO problems, you fucking pussy!"

Zip sat there quietly. He wasn't stunned by the tongue lashing. It was all true and he knew it.

"Look, I'm sorry," Street continued. "I've had a rough few days. Now my *good* arm is starting to fail me. I'm fat as fuck cuz I love food and I can't work out. I tried Ozempic, but all I did was just crap my pants so I stopped. Lord knows I've put Anna through enough, let alone having to wipe my ass, so I don't want to hear it. Put your fucking head down and kick that shit!"

"You're right," was all that Zip could muster.

Zip's doorbell rang. "Hold on a second, someone's at the door."

"No, I gotta go. I've got a zoom call with my therapist," Street replied. "She's going to earn her money today, boy. I already feel sorry for her."

He abruptly hung up.

"Hey, buddy," Elliott greeted, as Zip opened the door. "This a bad time?"

Zip thought about the question. He thought about the exchange he'd just had with Street. If there ever was a bad time this could be considered it. But Elliot rarely made house calls to Zip's house, so he figured it was something important.

"Absolutely not. Never a bad time, Elliot. Whatcha got there?" he said, noticing the bags that Elliot held in each hand.

"Well, there's rumblings that you and Biggs are on to something and I told you I wanted in. The way I see it, I helped. Well, myself and Rusty. So we want to back you guys. Rusty hasn't even looked at a heifer since, so I think he's got feelings for Biggs," he joshed.

Elliot reached into his bags and produced a couple of golf shirts, pullovers, some hats, and at least six dozen Pro V1 golf balls. Every item was either red or white with a caricature of a bull's head on the left side of the shirts over the heart and on the center of the hats. He had white colors with a red insignia and red colors with a white insignia. On the upper sleeves read the name RustyStone Ranch. On each golf ball, just like the clothing, was a small stamp of Rusty's head.

"Are you serious? RustyStone Ranch?" Zip asked Elliot.

"Absolutely, I'm dead serious. Why does Yellowstone get to have all the fun? Let's make my Ranch famous."

"This is amazing, Elliot. What's the catch?"

"Not a damn thing. Maybe I'll get in the organic meat game. Just a hobby cuz I don't need the money. That is, if Rusty can find a taste in heifers. Oh, and before I go, here ya go."

Elliott reached out and handed Zip a check, payable to him, for $25,000. "Whoa," Zip stammered. "I don't know what to say."

"I'd imagine you guys have some bills to pay while you prepare. I want total commitment, total focus. Not only on Biggs getting to the US Open but you getting him there," Elliott continued.

Zip began to choke up right there on his front porch. In the past, such a large commission or bonus check would prompt him to immediately call JD to put in an order. He wasn't a religious man. But with the conversation and subsequent dressing down he'd just had with Street, and now this incredibly generous outpouring from Elliot, it seemed something cosmic had occurred.

"I chose red because it's Rusty's favorite color, " Elliot laughed. "I hope it's not misconstrued with anyone that wears that color."

"Well, from what I've seen with Biggs, he's married and let's just say his marriage is a challenge right now. I'd be willing to bet that for new schwag and brand new Pro Vs he'd wear pink polka dots. But let's put it this way, his love for his wife is incredibly impressive. He's definitely not checkin' the menu at the Waffle House if you know what I mean. I've got a lot of respect for him and not just cuz he can spin a wedge like a magician. You'll see a real man wearing red. Thank you, Elliot."

To say Zip was conflicted this morning was an understatement. On one hand he couldn't wait to show Biggs the merch Elliot had provided along with the seed money. But on the other, he hadn't seen Biggs since the night Biggs stormed out of his house after literally catching him with a handful of painkillers. Neither had spoken to each other, so Zip decided to test the temperature of the situation and see if Biggs wanted to continue working with him. As he drove his cart towards Biggs' home for what he hoped would be a solid day of practice, he texted Biggs to get a sense of how pissed he still was.

*How you feeling today, big dog?*

*Waitin' on you, bro,* was the quick response that gave Zip a breath of relief.

Biggs hopped in Zip's cart almost before he could come to a complete stop.

"What are we working on today? I'm pumped."

"Really? What's going on?" Zip curiously asked.

"Nothing, just excited to work."

"How's things? How's Jessica?" Zip asked. He was eager to get a feel for his player's headspace as well as break any degree of awkwardness between the two of them.

"Well, to be honest, not much has changed though I mentioned that we're working together. It seemed to breathe a bit of life into her. We could really use some positive vibes," Biggs replied, as they drove towards the practice range.

"Are we pounding driver today with Rusty? Is he ready to pound me if I hit shitty shots?"

"Well, you know what they say," Zip answered, "'drive for show, putt for dough.' Actually, short game for dough. Today is short game . . . and as far as what you saw—"

"Hey listen, Zip," Biggs interrupted, "I told you I wouldn't mention it. I want to move on. But more importantly I want you to get it together. Okay?"

"I know, I am. I mean, I will. After today I need you to work on your own for a week or so. I'm going dark. Radio silence. I've been wanting to kick this shit a *long* time now. I can't let you, Maggie, Jessica, down. Shit, I even feel indebted to LH and the boys. I sound like a broken record but we can do this. I've asked a lot of you and I need to ask the same of myself. Shit, even more. I've done some reading about the withdrawal when you're kicking pills. Sure, I might shit my pants but I'm going to bear down and get through it. Now grab your sand wedge. We're headed for a day at the beach."

Zip walked around to the back of the golf cart and pulled a large pink piggy bank that belonged to Maggie from the basket attached to the back.

"What's that for? Does the ball machine only take quarters?" Biggs joked.

"Let me see your wedge," Zip asked and grabbed the club from Biggs' hand. "Follow me."

They walked over to a practice bunker that adorned a large practice green on the edge of the driving range. Zip placed Maggie's piggy bank on the grass at the edge of the bunker. He raised the wedge he was holding above his head and with a swift chop broke the ceramic pig in two pieces sending its head rolling down the grass hill while spilling its belly full of coins into the grass.

"Not sure Maggie's going to be too happy with that move," Biggs chuckled.

Zip reached down and grabbed the handful of coins. He placed some pennies in various areas of the bunker separating them by about a foot. He placed some dimes in the flatter areas and placed the pennies in uphill and downhill parts of the bunker. Some he even pushed deep into the sand and were barely visible.

"Great bunker players have great hands. Hands like a Catholic priest, some might say. I want you to envision these coins as if they were balls. Pop them outta the bunker and land them on the green. And don't bitch cuz I might make you stay in this bunker till you can land every one of them with their tails up."

"Gotcha," Biggs answered flatly.

At this point he was not going to question anything Zip instructed. He stepped into the bunker and methodically started digging the dimes and pennies out, one after the other. At first this drill was extremely challenging. He left his first handful of coins only a foot or so from their original position. However, he soon began to get into a beautiful rhythm and started flipping the coins onto the green with grace. After he'd hit six or seven, Zip raked the spots Biggs had been standing and proceeded to drop new coins there. This unorthodox activity drew the attention of practically everyone as they stopped hitting balls and watched with curiosity. After what seemed to be about $10 worth of coins, Zip instructed Biggs to stop and meet him on the practice green with his putter.

"Are we going to use actual balls or did Maggie also have a collection of marbles you're going to pull out?"

"Oh, you're going to enjoy this one, smart ass. Lift up your shirt."

"You going to make me put on a bra? Because after that session in front of the Cal women I could give a shit about being embarrassed."

"You see? It's working," Zip said. "No, keep your shirt on, just pull up the front."

Zip attached some round, plastic, stickers on each of Biggs' nipples. Each sticker had a small wire attached that was long enough to run from Biggs' nipples down along his side and out from under the back of his shirt. These wires attached to a square, black handheld box about the size of a cell phone. The device was equipped with what looked like a dial on the center that could be rotated.

"Come on, bro. What are you going to do with that thing?"

"It's simple actually," Zip grinned. "We're going to get you zeroed in on your putting. You see this dial? It's low voltage on the left. But when I turn it to the right . . . ZAP!"

Zip turned the dial a bit to the right and gave Biggs a little demonstration.

"Goddamn it!  That fucking HURTS, bro," Biggs screamed.

"Well, like many of the drills I've put you through, I'd suggest you concentrate," Zip said impishly. "I'll be gentle with the longer putts, but if I were you I wouldn't miss a shorty."

The next half hour was a sight to bewilder. A few of the folks that had been hitting range balls curiously walked over after witnessing Zip set balls down at various spots on the green and then take his position behind Biggs. Biggs would focus, go through his pre-putt routine, read the putt, breathe his last exhale, and pray he'd either drain the putt or leave it on the edge of the hole. He figured if it was on the edge, Zip might show some kindness and not zap him as hard. The other people, not knowing what was happening, only saw Biggs jumping and screaming vulgarities with each putt he missed.  A few wondered if a swarm of wasps had somehow infiltrated his shirt.  After Biggs had been zapped about a dozen times, his focus improved and his percentage of made putts greatly increased.

"Attaboy," Zip jeered. "Looks like you're getting 'dialed' in."

"I'll tell you what you can do with your dial," Biggs seethed.

"Okay here's the deal," Zip said. He placed a ball on the green in a precarious spot.

Roughly eight to ten people had stopped hitting balls and gathered around the practice green, clearly enjoying the antics. They cheered when Biggs made putts and laughed when he screamed and cried out after being zapped. The ball Zip placed on the green was about four feet from the cup. It was a severe downhill breaker.

"This is the one," Zip continued, "the four-foot downhill slider, severe break, to win The Masters. You make it, we're done. You're the champ. You miss it and sparks might fly from your shirt."

A hush came over the small but enthused gallery.

"Come on, Biggs," one of them called out.

Biggs stopped his pre-putt routine. He looked up at the small group of spectators, recognized the hush, smiled at them shrewdly, looked down at his ball, and slowly stroked a putt that started far outside the hole before curling back and stopping. It dangled on the edge of the hole for what seemed like a minute.  Zip reached for the dial on his zapper just as the ball gracefully dropped down to the bottom of the cup. The tiny crowd erupted as if they were standing on the 18th at Augusta instead of this meager practice area at Eagle Vista. With one quick and violent motion Biggs raised his arms in elation and then reached under his shirt and ripped off the pasties.

"Zip, let's get the fuck outta here!"

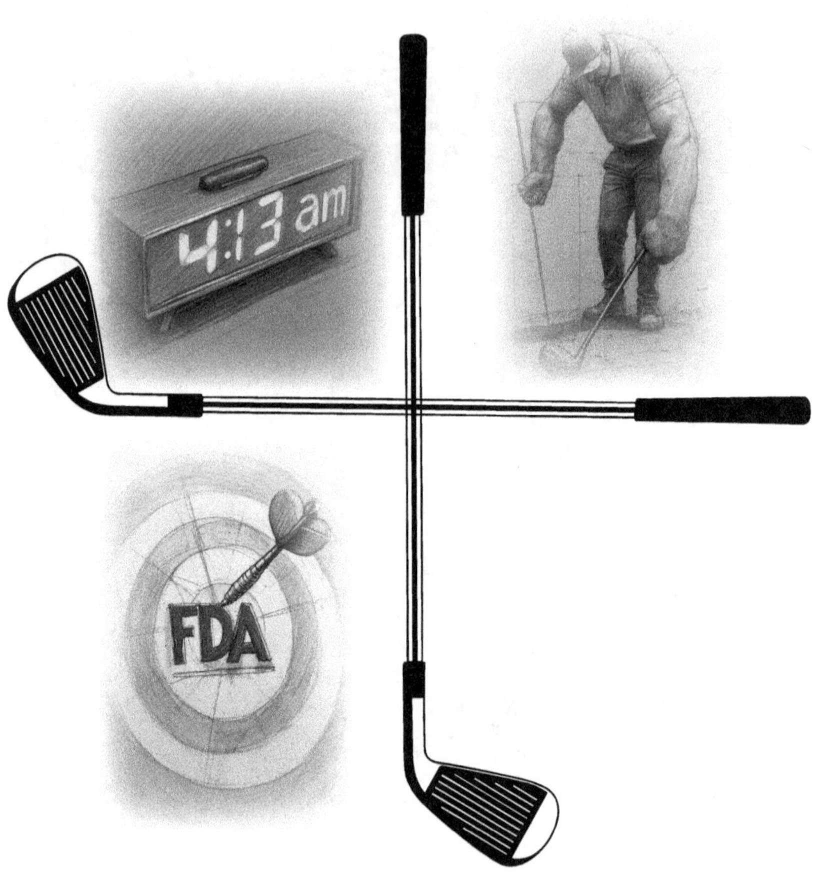
4:13 am
FDA

## HOLE #15

Zip rolled over in bed and checked his phone that read: 4:13 a.m. He hadn't slept a minute. In fact, this was the third night in a row the insomnia from his opioid detox had prevented him from getting an ounce of sleep. He'd be totally exhausted when he'd crawl into bed around 10:00 p.m. But from there he'd toss and turn, flopping around like a fish out of water. After those initial difficult nights, he would be able to finally fall asleep around 5:00 a.m. But after two or three hours he'd wake up in a sweat-soaked shirt that looked like he'd jumped in a swimming pool. The tiny clock on his nightstand beamed like a giant, torturous, digital billboard constantly reminding him of the hours that passed and the sleep he wasn't getting. He was doing it though. He was determined to get the opioid poison out of his system no matter how many shirts he drenched.

One morning he stood in his front yard watering the lawn and plants that were on the verge of dying from his neglect. It must have been a Tuesday because the garbage truck drove by. He chuckled at how quietly his garbage can emptied into the truck. He couldn't believe he was actually awake to witness the truck driving by. How many mornings had he been under the covers while the truck emptied all of his empty bottles and cans with a thunderous crash?

*How you feeling?* his phone pinged. It was Street, who besides Biggs, was the only other person Zip had told of his commitment to detoxing.

*Well, I don't wanna bitch. Obviously, I did this to myself and it's not in the same ballpark as the fight that you're dealing with,* Zip typed.

*No, it's fine. I like it when others suffer too,* Street responded with a ☺ .

Zip then called Street rather than continuing to text back and forth.

"Jesus, must be important," Street said, as he answered.

"I figured I better tell you about it because any second I could be running to the can before I shit my pants. I've had absolutely nothing solid for days now. I haven't slept. My muscles are twitching like crazy at night."

"Oh, that's great! Now you know how I feel . . . every freaking day!"

They both laughed.

"I'm getting it out of me though," Zip continued. "You'll love this. I was reading where microdosing mushrooms can alleviate some of the withdrawal symp—"

"STOP! That's all you need!" Street barked, cutting Zip off mid-sentence. "More shit to put in your body. Did it work?"

"Well, yes and no. I mean I melted into my couch watching a golf tournament on TV. I may have macrodosed instead of microdosed. I had no idea how much to take and I didn't feel anything, so I took more doses and . . . good lord! Within fifteen minutes I swear Bryson DeChambeau's forearms looked like Popeye on steroids. They seemed to be inflating right there in front of me. So, yeah, I forgot about the discomfort of detoxing for a while but on the other hand I was TRIPPIN'.  My skin felt like it was crawling at night and I twitched like I have Tourette's. But we've got the first qualifier tournament coming up in about a week. I'll make it. How are you feeling?"

Obviously trying to kick an atrocious drug and alcohol addiction was nowhere near the scale of suffering from multiple sclerosis. But Zip felt a connection with Street. His predicament was self-induced and, if he kept at it, curable. But they were both suffering at the same time and Zip definitely sensed that Street felt a bit of joy that someone else felt as shitty as he did practically every day.

"I'm okay," Street responded, with his normal rehearsed response. "I read on my MS site there's a company that has a drug in a Stage 2 trial. Supposedly slows down the progression. I've seen this shit so many times though. These drug companies spit out promising results and get a bunch of investors to fund them a while longer. But it all turns out to be bullshit in the end. It's too late for me. By the time they get to a Stage 3 trial, and that's a huge if, the FDA will drag their fucking feet approving anything. The FDA sucks. I'm going to die in this chair."

"I'm sorry, man. I really am."

All Zip could do was respond as well with his normal canned reply he'd said many times. But he really meant it. It broke his heart to see how this disease had destroyed his friend. A phone call beeped on the other line. It was Biggs. Zip hadn't heard from him since he'd electrocuted him.

"Hey, I've got to take this call," Zip told Street.

"Yeah, no problem. My physical therapist will be here any minute now. He's going to yell at me for not doing my exercises but he can go fuck himself. He thinks he's a big motivator but try living in my shoes. I'm paying $300 an hour to get belittled."

"Okay, well, have fun with that," Zip snickered, as he switched over to Biggs. "How you doing, Biggs?"

"Super, bro, I've been practicing every day. Even played a round yesterday with zero music. Just the sounds of the occasional crow. You know what? I liked it. I've been looking at Sacramento CC online too. I'm ready, man. More importantly, how are you feeling?"

"I'm good, man. Other than occasionally crapping my drawers, I'm in uncharted waters as far as days without junk. We're going to do this. I guess 80 or so players have signed up and all we need to do is be in the top four. Once I get a decent night's sleep, I'm going to go out to SAC CC and walk the place. Do some charting. But your game fits the place well. I don't want you to come with me though. We need to be spontaneous. In the moment. Focused without noise. If we're prepped too much and you think too much, it'll take away from your creative genius. No fucking rabbit ears!"

"No one's ever called me genius!" cracked Biggs. "But I have definitely learned a thing or four about focus and pain tolerance."

"Saturday. Be ready to rock," was Zip's simple directive.

16

## HOLE #16

Biggs woke up before his alarm could sound. He checked his phone. There was a simple text from Zip asking if he was awake. Biggs had trouble sleeping but by the looks of the text that came in at 4:00 a.m., it was apparent that Zip had similar trouble.

*Yeah, I'm getting coffee going. Why you up so early?* Biggs tapped back.

*Not up early, more like haven't slept. I've kicked much of the withdrawal but the insomnia still lingers. Anyway, make a small cup. Let's get going. The tourney doesn't start for a few hours but I'll buy you breakfast in Sacramento and we can go over my course layout and notes in my yardage book,* Zip texted.

Biggs was more than ready. He had also written some notes that he wanted to share with Zip. He was quietly assembling the golf attire that he wanted to wear when Jessica rolled over in bed to see what he was doing.

"Oh shit, sorry I woke you, hun," he said.

"Is today the day?" she asked in a sleep-filled voice.

"Today's one of the days, babe. I need to play well to advance to the next qualifier. I feel good though. Go back to sleep."

Jessica got out of bed and gave her husband a long hug. Zip's car honked politely out front. It was still dark. Not even the birds were chirping.
"Be great today, Thomas. I believe in you," Jessica whispered.

"How are you feeling? Nervous?" Zip asked when Biggs jumped in the front seat.

"Not nervous. Anxious is more like it. Looks like you are too? The tourney doesn't even start until 10:00 a.m. I guess we'll have plenty of time to prep," Biggs joked.

The drive to Sacramento was about an hour and a half. As they approached the outskirts of town, Zip pulled into a truck stop next to the freeway.

"These joints always make the best breakfast," he told Biggs. "By the way, where'd you get that shirt and hat?"

"You like?" Biggs snickered. "Look, this is all I have that is halfway decent."

"What the fuck is that logo, Happy Trails? Is that a course you used to play?"

"No, Happy Trails was a marijuana dispensary that went out of business. They used to sponsor me when I played Korn Ferry. They were the only sponsor that offered me any money, actually, more like product. They gave me a little scratch but mostly paid me in vape pens and gummies. I was constantly stoned. Just another of the many reasons I never made the tour."

"Well, I've got good news," Zip replied. "We are upgrading you from a weed store to a ranch with a gay bull."

Zip reached in the back seat and pulled out a bag with the shirts, hats, pants, and windbreaker, that Elliot had given him.

"You shittin' me?!" Biggs exclaimed, as he opened the beautiful red shirt with Rusty's silhouette stenciled over the chest and on the front of the hat. "This is amazing. What's this?" he asked, pointing to an emblem on the sleeve that read: <u>MSR.com</u>.

"I added that," Zip said. "It's a website for a research laboratory that specializes in multiple sclerosis. I'm hoping you play well enough that we get some attention towards helping folks with MS."

"Not that I don't have enough pressure on me. Between a wife that won't get out of bed and a bull that wants me to stroke his giant cock, now I got to play well for people suffering with MS?" Biggs shrugged.

"Oh, don't forget about me. You need to do this for an old broken down caddy as well," Zip chuckled. "Now go get changed."

Biggs hurried into the truck stop's restroom holding the bag of assorted merch. He practically ripped off the ratty Happy Trails shirt in the middle of the diner; he was so excited about what choices to wear.

The waitress came over to give them their bill.

"You boys enjoy your breakfast? You barely touched your short stack, hun."

"No, everything was fine. Just some stomach issues. We need to get going anyway. Need to get to the Sacramento Country Club. Do you know the place? Isn't it up the freeway a bit, off to the left?" Zip asked her.

"Yes, it is, honey. But you won't have any problems. All the traffic behind you coming from the Bay Area is shut down. One of these boys in here said an 18-wheeler full of Coca-Cola flipped over a ways back. Spread Coke bottles across all the lanes. It'll take them hours to clean that ole mess," she said, snapping her gum between every word.

"You gotta be fucking kidding me!" Zip barked, just as Biggs approached the table.

"How do I loo—" Biggs stopped mid-sentence. "What's going on?"

"Shit, I guess the freeway's blocked a few miles back. There's a lot of players coming from the Bay Area. They're going to be screwed. Let's get to the course," Zip said, as he jumped up from the table.

They pulled into the roundabout at Sac CC and immediately noticed a huddle of tournament organizers and rules officials in serious talks just outside the club's double doors. There were a few players that had checked in and were holding their tournament kits, but for a field this size it definitely looked well short of participants. Zip approached a woman seated behind the check-in table.

"We heard about the truck accident. Is the tournament still on?" he anxiously asked.

"Oh, yes, sir," she calmly informed him. "We have to play. We're on a tight schedule as it is. But we've had lots of local players and players from the Nevada area make it. We'll have to figure out what to do for those players that are stuck, but for those that are here we've made a few adjustments. Instead of an 82-man field with the top four advancing we've got about 40 players so only the top two will advance. The range is around to the right. We're ready to go on time, so go ahead and get ready. Here's your kit."

Zip pulled out the scorecard and local rules pamphlet to put in his yardage book. He handed a scorecard to Biggs, who pulled out his own yardage book from his back pocket of his sleek new golf pants that Elliot provided. As he opened his book there was a handwritten note tucked into the slot where the scorecard went. It was from Jessica.

*Babe, I'm sorry for how things have been,* the note read. *You are an inspiration. I'm getting out of this bed. I will be everything you need me to be. Perhaps we try for another baby. KICK ASS!*

Biggs immediately felt like a huge apple had wedged in his throat as he began to choke up. He looked up from reading the note and looked at his caddy although Zip could see that his player wasn't looking at him but through him and in a tranquil, composed voice said, "Zip, these motherfuckers are going down."

News had spread through the field about the freeway mess. All anyone could talk about was how the field had been basically cut in half and only two players would advance instead of the original four. Biggs however couldn't care less as he and Zip went through their preparation routine on the putting green. The note from Jessica had Biggs amped and ready. A local TV crew was interviewing a player just off the side of the practice green which seemed odd because this was a local qualifier with mostly no names and not much fanfare.

"What's with this guy?" Zip asked, referring to the player being interviewed.

"That's Myron Pitts, played with him on KF, total jabroni. His dad runs a huge hedge fund. He could basically give a shit about golf cuz he knows he's going to be filthy rich. Lives in the area which is probably why the news gives a shit. I've had some run-ins with him on KF because I was playing for livelihood and he was an arrogant ass," Biggs explained to Zip.

Zip ventured over towards the interview. He walked in the background of the camera shot and mouthed a "Hi, Maggie" with a goofy look on his face that prompted the reporter to sternly ask him to get the fuck out of her shot.

"What do you think your chances are today, Myron?" the reporter asked.

"Well, if I can hit fairways and greens, I think I'll have a good shot to contend," Myron replied, with his hands on his hips as if he was posing for an interview on the Golf Channel.

"Captain Obvious," Zip blurted out, loud enough to be heard.

"Hey, for the last time, get the hell out of my shot!" the reporter demanded.

Myron gave Zip a dagger look. "Is that your boy over there?" Myron motioned towards Biggs, who was continuing to putt. "You might wanna keep the car running. Used to call him Sylvester on Korn Ferry because coming down the stretch he'd choke harder than a cat swallowing a furball."

Myron tossed this insulting grenade towards Biggs loud enough so all of the fellow golfers around the putting green could hear, which garnered a cumulative roar of laughter. The reporter was also amused.

Biggs looked over, grabbed his crotch, and calmly said, "Hey, Myron, choke on this," producing an equal roar.

Suddenly it felt as if the normal sportsmanship etiquette that usually accompanies golf tournaments had taken a turn towards a weigh in at a boxing match. With half the field screwed by the misfortune of being stuck behind a thousand broken Coke bottles strewn across the highway, these two rivals had definitely livened up a downtrodden atmosphere.

"Listen, it's a beautiful day for golf," Myron spoke into the microphone, trying to ignore Biggs' comeback. "I owe everything to my Lord and Savior Jesus Christ and with his guidance I hope to have his power to play well."

The first hole was a short par 4 lined with fairway bunkers that called for accuracy. Zip pulled out a 3 wood for Biggs to hit. His notes told him that, much like Eagle Vista, the hole was short and tight.

"Let's start conservative, hit the fairway. We can try for a birdie with the second shot," he told Biggs, as he handed him the club.

"Fuck that!" Biggs countered.

Biggs pulled the driver from his bag and literally tattooed his first shot of the day that carried some 325 yards, avoided all the bunker trouble, and rolled out to about 350 yards, dead center of the fairway. His second shot was a mere 30 yards to the pin. The kind of shot Biggs had hit thousands of times. However, he was so pumped up he hammered his 60 degree wedge and sailed the ball well over the green, landing it some 75 yards away.

"Jesus, kid, calm the fuck down! I know Jess' note got you pumped but let's stay within yourself. It's a long day out here and we got 18 of these. Breathe, my man, breathe," Zip barked.

"Sorry. Shit. Sorry, it's that cocksucker Myron too. He pisses me off." Biggs inhaled a long deep breath and tried to exhale all of his excitement.

"There you go, buddy. Get the bad air out," Zip sternly directed his player. "I hear you. But we got to play the course today, not him. Beat the course. Screw Myron. He'll choke on that silver spoon. I heard him talking about God being with him, so let's just hope God's dealing with one of the OTHER 8 billion people on earth with more pressing needs. Hopefully, he's a little too busy to be paying attention to Myron today."

"I don't know but it feels like these balls are just launching off my club face. Do you have any of those softer Kirklands from Costco? Maybe I can dial those down a bit," Biggs inquired.

"Can't switch. I read the local rules the lady at the table handed me. We got to play the same brand of ball we started with. Trust me, it ain't the ball or the clubs. It's the Indian not the arrow. Just calm down. We play for par and let the birdies fall where they may. Remember they can move the flags but they can't move the middle of the green. Tap in par, take 'em ALL DAY," Zip instructed Biggs in a reassuring tone to which he felt a bit at ease.

"I wish I had some of those Happy Trails gummies to mellow me out but I gotta say that Elliott's schwag looks fantastic. Look good, play good, right?"

Throughout the next couple of hours Biggs played beautifully. He took what the course gave him and listened to Zip's instructions. The two of them created a nice rhythm but, as with any round of golf, they would be tested. On the 7th hole, his approach shot to the green had a high arcing trajectory when a gust of wind halted his ball from reaching the green and sent it plunging deep into the sand of a green side bunker. The sand was deep in this particular area and the height of the shot buried the ball so that only the top was visible. This was a perfect example of why these types of results were called fried eggs. They were difficult situations and often led to disastrous blow up holes. As Zip evaluated the situation, he grabbed the 60 degree wedge and handed it to Biggs.

"Damn, we got hosed. Forget par. Just get it to the green and we'll take a bogey," he instructed Biggs.

"We didn't break Maggie's piggy bank to make bogeys." And with that comment Biggs confidently dug the ball out from its plugged spot landing it a few feet from the hole and saved par.

On the 12th green, they had a 20-foot curler for birdie. The putt was downhill and had a severe left to right break and if hit too hard could easily roll off the green. Zip had noticed that Biggs was wearing a thick rubber band around his wrist and as they lined up his putt, Biggs pulled on the rubber band and let it snap crisply onto the tender part of his skin under his wrist a few times.

"What's that all about?" Zip asked.

"It snaps me into focus. Kinda like an electric shock if I miss," he smirked, clearly referring to Zip's nipple drill.

He stood over the ball and with a fluid stroke precisely drained the difficult putt. They played the round with no music and no noise to speak of.  The crowds were no more than a handful of people. Mostly family members that followed their particular player. In Zip's eyes, Biggs handled the round like a champ. He finished the round at 6 under par. Tied with one other player for second place. Obviously only two would advance due to the field being reduced. As a result, there would be a sudden death playoff with the other player that Biggs tied and, as the golf gods would have it, that player was none other than Myron Pitts. Myron had finished his round about a half an hour before Biggs and was staying loose on the driving range.

"You want to hit some balls on the range before the playoff?" Zip asked his guy.

Myron walked over towards them. "Been waiting on you, Sylvester. You ready?" he smugly asked.

Biggs turned toward Zip and before Zip could hand him a club to hit a few balls to stay loose, Biggs said, "Fuck the range, let's get this punk!"

The first playoff hole was an easy par 4 to which both players made par. The next playoff hole was a long par 3 over a pond. Biggs led off. He stood over his ball for what felt like an awkwardly long time. There was dead silence until a fire truck, sirens blaring, could be heard in the distance. Biggs' rabbit ears were creeping into his psyche and he was desperate to not get distracted. Zip walked over and stopped him from hitting.

"Reset. Go through your routine again."

Biggs again went through his pre-shot routine. He inhaled and exhaled letting the bad air out. He addressed his ball and, with his customary, fluid swing, inexplicably dunked his shot directly into the middle of the pond. Myron pretended to cough a bit like he had something stuck in his throat obviously referencing that Biggs had choked. It was a chickenshit gesture that didn't go unnoticed by Zip. Myron placed his ball on his tee, arrogantly smirked, and  promptly replicated Biggs' hack sending his ball into the pond as well.

"Where's God when you need him?" Zip muttered to Myron, as they all walked towards the drop zone.

Zip's comment irritated Myron so much that he shanked his next shot from the drop area into a green side bunker. Biggs, however, hit a beautiful shot that landed about five feet from the pin. He was so excited he could barely contain himself. He was clearly in the driver's seat. What happened next could only be chalked up to that familiar phrase that echoes when a golfer witnesses something extraordinary. And usually when he thinks he's got the advantage. Quite simply, "That's golf."

Myron's bunker shot sculled off the bottom of his wedge, screamed across the green, and smacked the flag stick with such velocity that the ball came to a dead stop and dropped straight into the hole. He'd saved bogey. Zip dropped his head in disbelief. Biggs now needed to make his five-footer to tie. Unfortunately, he left his attempt on the edge of the cup. Made double. Lost. He dropped his putter, bent over with both hands on his knees, and just froze in utter agony. His stomach sank as he realized Myron was moving on to the next qualifier and he and Zip were going home.

An elated Myron came over to shake both Biggs' and Zip's hand and then, like he'd just won the Masters, tossed his ball to a few kids off to the side of the green. Biggs just stared at the ground, totally devastated. As Myron tossed his ball, Zip saw the kid that caught it show it to his friend. Zip wasn't certain but he thought he saw a red number on the ball in the kid's hand.

"Hey, kid, let me see that ball for a second," he asked the boy.

And sure as Rusty's bullshit, the ball the kid was holding was a Titleist Pro V1x with a red number. Not the black numbered Pro V1 that Myron had teed off with on the par 3.

"Oh, Myron," Zip proclaimed, "we got an issue here. This isn't the same type of ball you started with and local rules say you got to play the same type of ball throughout the round."

"What?! That's ridiculous! After we hit it in the water, I pulled a new Titleist from my bag. What difference does it make if it's a Pro V1 or Pro V1x?!" Myron protested.

Biggs had finally looked up from his defeated pose and was curious as to what all the commotion his caddy had started was about. A rules official was standing right there. He took a long look at the ball, conferred with some other officials and confirmed that indeed Myron had played his entire round, including starting sudden death, with a black numbered Titleist Pro V1. Playing any part of the round with a different type of ball, even though it was the same brand, constituted an infraction that resulted in a penalty. And just like that Myron was penalized two strokes resulting in him finishing the hole with a 6 to Biggs' 5. Biggs was awarded second place all to himself and would now be moving on to the next qualifier. Biggs and Zip showed some class. They didn't embrace. They didn't celebrate. They simply walked to their car hiding their elation. They knew they'd won on a technicality but they both could care less.

When they got to the trunk of the car, Biggs embraced Zip with a huge hug. "You're fucking amazing, bro! I never saw any difference in his ball! Let's get drunk. In fact, I'm buying dinner. A special dinner. We always have to hear about the champions dinner at the fucking Masters like we give a shit. This dinner is going to be more like a feast a death row prisoner gets. All out! Tell Maggie to come. I doubt I can get Jess outta bed but I gotta call her," he said, as tears flowed down his cheeks.

"Sounds great. But look, this is just step one, okay. Let's process this and celebrate this day. But we have much bigger goals ahead," Zip said, with a soothing demeanor.

The drive home took them through rural Sacramento. Steak joints lined the road advertising T-bones, prime rib, rib eyes, porterhouses, the full meat and baked potato gamut. Biggs peered out the passenger side window like a 10-year-old kid and studied each and every billboard promoting the various restaurants. His mood was so joyful he actually emulated that 10-year-old, so excited that he was about to stop and eat at a fancy restaurant.

"How's a fat steak sound?"

"I'm not a huge health nut, definitely not a vegan, or the liberal I'm labeled by everyone for simply attending Berkeley, but how about a seafood place?" Zip replied. "I just have a hard time eating chicken or steak. Something about ingesting an animal that stands around in their own shit all day turns me off. Don't even start about organic ranches either. They've had investigations that proved the livestock at those places are raised horribly."

"Now you actually *do* sound like a Berkeley liberal," Biggs shot back. "Fine, seafood it is. Jess isn't answering me. I can't wait to tell her."

"Send Maggie a text. Tell her to join us at Spengers. They have a great bar where we can wait for a table," Zip instructed Biggs and added, "neither of us is driving home from there."

Spengers had been around for almost a century. It sat at the edge of the San Francisco Bay in Berkeley. Fishermen used to bring their haul from the Pacific right up to the Spengers' loading dock that sat at the water's edge. The bar was a long oak slab of wood covered in a thick varnish that protected old photos of grizzly men standing on their boats loading huge salmon, bass, sturgeon, and crab onto the dock that led to the restaurant. A gigantic marlin hung over the bar. It was a bit out of place as no marlin swam in the local waters, but folks were there to dine, not question the authenticity of the decor.

"Words can't describe how I'm feeling," Biggs said, as he sat practically in disbelief with a cold draft beer and stared into the fake eyes of the marlin.

"I wish Jess was there. You have no idea what getting back on tour would do for us. We need money. I need to get her into therapy. I know we've got tons of work to do but I know I can put myself into contention again. And you know what? I couldn't tell you if it was noisy or stone cold silent out there, Zip. I was just so focused. I can't express to you—"

"That's enough of that. We haven't done a goddamn thing yet," Zip snarled. "The only thing we know is we're moving on to Harding for the 36-hole final qualifier. The other thing we know is we're going to get hammered right here right now. But you've also helped me more than you know."

Zip's phone pinged from a text Maggie sent: *Going to be late, Dad. I had to call roadside. I'm in the school parking lot. Tires all flat. Pretty sure Jake had something to do with it.*

"That fucking little cocksucker!" Zip snapped. "Is it legal to beat an 18-year-old?"

"What's up?" Biggs queried.

Before Zip could lash out about Maggie's predicament and who they assumed caused it, the bartender approached and informed them that their table was ready.

"Gentlemen, do you know what you'll be eating? I'll send an appropriate wine bottle to your table."

"We're going with halibut and salmon. Also, my daughter's on her way but we may need to get hers to go. She likes the swordfish with a bowl of your clam chowder," Zip announced in the same commanding fashion he might instruct Biggs to select a particular golf club. "Oh, and send two bottles."

*Roadside just pulled up. Be there as soon as possible. Don't wait at the bar as I don't want to have to pour both of you into the car later,* Maggie texted, adding a ☺.

Over the course of the next half hour Zip and Biggs ate, drank, and definitely got merry. They evaluated the day's events. They toasted every great shot and putt. They talked about the layout at Harding Park. Outlined their preparation. They even detailed which outfit that Elliott provided would look best on Biggs. Then oddly, Zip's phone rang with an incoming FaceTime call from Street. Street had never FaceTimed Zip before so he figured that Street had obviously butt dialed him by mistake. He was in a good mood so Zip propped his phone against a candle and accepted the call. Street was also surprised to now be staring at the two of them at their table.

"What the hell?" Street said.

"Hey, buddy, it's me and meet Biggs. You butt dialed me by mistake. We just had a fantastic day. Biggs qualified for the next round."

"No kidding?! Congratulations, Biggs. I've heard many great things about you."

"Thank you, sir. I couldn'—"

"But do me a favor," Street interrupted, "take good care of him cuz I'm going to need him back after your little field trip. He does a lot for me."

"I do a lot for *you*? No, you've got that wrong. You do a *ton* for me," Zip stammered drunkenly.

"Oh, I like this, this is getting mushy. Mr. Street, if you don't mind, give me an example of how Zip helps you?" Biggs chimed in.

There was a long pause as they all seemed to get a bit serious. The alcohol may have enhanced the sentimentality of the moment, but their eyes all glanced at each other in anticipation of what someone might say.

"Well, let me put it this way," Street started. "I've never known someone so empathetic and sensitive to what I'm going through. He never tells me what I should be doing to get better. Doesn't give me advice because he understands that until you walk in my shoes you don't have a clue.

He never tells me when he's doing things he knows I can no longer do because he doesn't want me to feel like I'm missing out. I know he won't admit this, but I just know him. My life is tough for sure. But he doesn't show any pity. He listens. And he makes me laugh like hell so I almost piss my pants right in my wheelchair."

"Well let's make sure that doesn't happen. And, Zip, what's Street do for you?" Biggs continued.

"Hey, we're supposed to be celebrating here. Not gettin' all Dr. Phil," Zip blurted out.

"No, I get it, Mr. Street. He's helped me immensely," Biggs jumped in. "No way on earth I'd be sitting here if it wasn't for Zip. I hope he understands how grateful—"

"Hey, the giant marlin on the wall is rolling his eyes. Enough, let's drink," Zip demanded.

"No, wait a minute," Biggs continued. "You've helped lift a heavy cloud that's hanging over my family. I want so bad to do this for Jessica, for you, Zip. I know we can do this together. I finally feel like the future is limitless again." "And you, Zip?" Street asked.

"I don't want to go full Cal psychology class on you guys. But I feel guilty. It breaks my heart to see you like this. I'm able-bodied and you are not and it's almost like I feel survivor's guilt for you. I've known you so long, Street, and we've shared so much life together and those memories are awesome, but I pray so badly that you could be that strong motherfucker you once were. I know I don't walk in your shoes but I walk beside you. As long as it takes."

And just like that, Street hung up. Perhaps the situation was getting too emotional and Street was fantastic at cutting off the moment at the perfect time. Biggs and Zip started another round of toasting. They were hugging and crying drunk tears of joy when Maggie showed up.

"Jesus, look at you two," she laughed. "Sorry, Dad, it was Jake. I saw him watching from his car the whole time. You were right, Dad. He's a mama's boy. I don't feel anything for him anymore."

"That's my Maggie," Zip slurred, as he turned to give her a huge hug. "I'll deal with that punk later."

"Dad, you smell!"

"It's been a long day, hun. Let's go. We'll get the car tomorrow."

Just then his phone pinged again. It was JD.  The text simply read: *Birds are flying,* which informed Zip that JD was stock full of pills. Zip was drunk and on any normal day being in this state and in a celebratory mood, he would have raced to JD's to pick up a supply of happy pills to keep the party rolling. But with a swift swipe of his thumb he deleted the text. He also deleted JD's contact info. He pushed the old wooden captain's wheels that acted as door handles attached to the exit doors of Spengers and paused for a moment. He inhaled a deep breath of fresh ocean air and gazed into the setting sun just beyond the Golden Gate Bridge. Biggs was not the only person to achieve an incredible milestone today. Zip had kicked his drug habit and wasn't going backwards.

As they walked to the car, he pulled both Biggs and Maggie into each side of his body. He put his arms around their shoulders and gratifyingly said,
"Let's go home."

*If you guys are in the area, stop by the club* was the text Zip received from LH. *CONGRATS* was the next ping.

"Looks like LH knows you advanced," Zip said to Biggs. "I'm sure he followed you around online. He asked us to stop at the club. Okay final final for real this time."

"I can go, but just for one quick one. I want to get home to Jess."

All the cast of characters were seated at the club bar. When Zip, Biggs, and Maggie walked in, a huge ovation broke out. The Commish came right up to Biggs to congratulate him and shake his hand.

"Way to go, Biggs! How does it feel?" the Commish offered.

"Well, it was a bit nerve—" Biggs tried to respond but was immediately interrupted.

"I remember when I got the call from the Dodgers," the Commish continued. "I was just so excited. There's no bigger thrill than finding out you're going to play a sport you love professionally."

"Thank you, Pete," Zip intervened.

He pulled Biggs away before he was about to be swarmed by a hornet's nest of the Commish's self-indulgence.

"Perhaps you can sign a ball for us later," Zip mocked.

Zip escorted Biggs through the throng of members that were eager to congratulate and glad-hand him. The members beamed with pride that one of their own had accomplished such a feat.

"Whatcha having?" rang out around the bar.

Everyone wanted to buy both of them a drink, not knowing they were already quite drunk. They grabbed a corner of the bar and bellied up. LH was next to approach, or rather barge into Biggs' personal space with his alcohol- soaked breath.

"You hit 10 outta 14 fairways, 28 putts in all. You hit 13 greens in regulation and your strokes gained were . . ." LH blathered on.

Zip again stepped in, putting his arm in between Biggs and LH to prevent LH from crowding Biggs and stop the barrage of numbers and stats that LH was about to inflict on Biggs. Navigating Biggs through the bar and protecting him from the barrage of inebriated offerings from the members, although well intended, was some of the best caddying Zip had done all day.

"Yes, thank you, LH, thank you. We'll look at the numbers in a bit but right now let's just celebrate," Zip politely told him.

"How'd you like the outfits?" Elliot asked, entering the fray.

"Oh, I can't thank you enough, Mr. Wallace. I felt great out there and with ole Rusty on my chest here, I was invincible," Biggs replied, tapping the logo of Rusty's head on his chest.

Elliot started handing cigars around the bar.

"We got lots to celebrate today, boys! I heard a ruckus in my barn and went to check and lo and behold my boy Rusty was mounting one of my heifers. Not sure what had come over him but perhaps he could sense ole Biggs' success and wanted to celebrate. I'm so proud of both my boys! Maybe we can move some meat someday."

Biggs was confused by Elliot's statement about moving meat. He hadn't yet heard of Elliot's organic meat endeavors.

"Well, sir, I don't know what that means but, yeah, I guess. As long as Rusty's happy."

"What's this MSR here on the sleeve?" Elliot asked

Zip intervened and said, "That's for my friend Street. I'm trying to get some attention for multiple sclerosis research. I hope you don't mind, Elliot. I added that."

"No, no, that's fantastic," Elliott added.

More and more members piled into the bar over the next hour. Word of the victory had gotten around. Everyone wanted to share this moment. There were plenty of handshakes and backslaps. Eagle Vista had never had a fellow member achieve such an accomplishment and they all wanted to show their appreciation. Biggs looked at Zip after a bit and tapped his wrist. He wasn't wearing a watch but it was the universal sign that he wanted to go. He showed Zip a text from Jessica.

*Where are you?* it read.

"Okay, let's get out of here," Zip said. "I have an early tee time at Harding tomorrow anyway. I'm going to scour that place mentally. Get us ready for a few weeks from now. And, crap, I got to get to Spengers first to get my car." He stood up off his barstool and put his in the air like a marshal trying to quiet a crowd around before a player hits.

"Listen, everyone, we want to thank you all so much for your support. It's only one step towards a larger goal. We've got another qualifier coming up and this love that you've shown will carry us along. But it's time to go." They exited to a chorus of "Good luck" and "Go get 'em."

Biggs walked into his house and the first thing he noticed was the amazing smell of freshly popped popcorn. Jess was not in bed. In fact, she was actually fully dressed. Her hair was styled and she was sitting on the couch holding a huge bowl filled with popcorn.

"What's all this? You okay?" he asked.

"Just want to know if you want to watch a movie, babe?" Jessica methodically asked, as if tonight was as normal as they'd once been.

"Goddamn right I do! Just let me get out of these clothes."

"No, it's okay honey. I like you just the way you are. I've been in my pj's for months so the least I care about is how you're dressed. But I do want to know what the hell this bull is about that's on your shirt?"

"Long story, hun . . . I'll tell you later," Biggs said, as he happily plopped down next to her on the couch.

It wasn't a monumental moment to have Jess out of bed. But, actually, Jess wanting to spend a simple evening with Biggs meant the world to him. Biggs was so curious as to why all of a sudden Jessica was present. Sure, he'd called her after the match and told her he won. But he didn't expect this. But something inside him told him not to delve. To just accept the moment and relish in its simplicity. It was so gratifying. He felt like they were back in their old studio with the stinky golf shoes. He didn't care how long it lasted. He knew in that pure moment he had her back. With all they had endured, regardless of today's awesome achievement, this quiet evening together was a perfect way to cap such a memorable day.

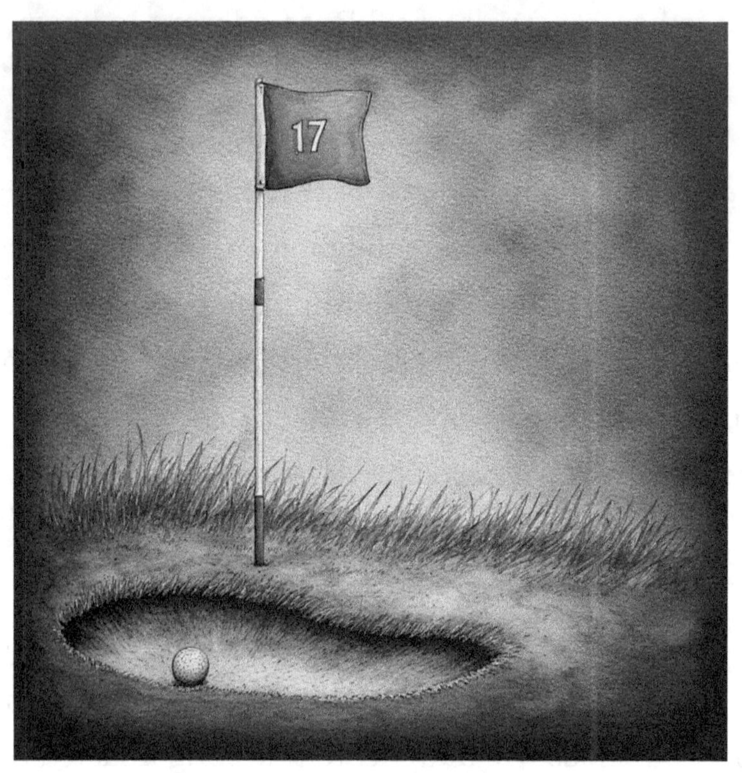

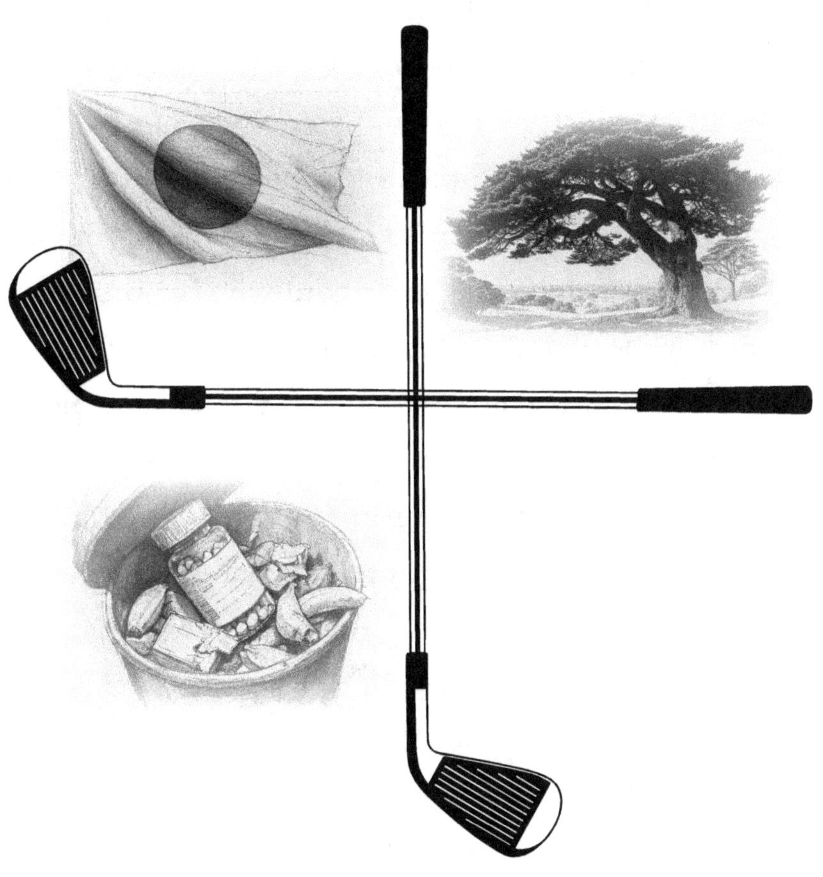

## HOLE #17

Zip ran to the first tee at Harding Park. Hungover and disheveled, he greeted the three Japanese gentlemen that he'd been paired with to play that morning. As he tucked in his shirt, he gestured some type of bow he hoped they'd see as an apology for being late. But, instead, the bow came across awkwardly inappropriate. Today, however, he cared less about who he was playing with or how he would be interpreted. This day was about studying the course. He wanted to look for nooks and crannies, bunkers, blind spots, trees that blocked greens. He wanted to discover and analyze anything he could to provide some insight as to where to hit the ball and, more importantly, where not to. Zip was a fairly decent player, but he was willing to sacrifice today's round. He would purposely hit shots into horrible roughs and then hit grounders on the fairways and into the green side bunkers in order to develop a strategy that could help Biggs when he played the course.

The Japanese guys had no idea what Zip was doing. They only saw a player, who, when it was his turn to hit, was god-awful. If Zip was 100 yards from a pin, he'd purposely hit a ball that sailed 125 yards over the green, just so he could play from the rough on the other side of the hole. He was determined to comb this golf course, shot after shot, regardless if it took him 125 shots to finish or made him look ridiculous doing it. His putting was atrocious. He'd purposely putt a ball well past a hole so it would end up on an up slope or a down slope allowing him to evaluate every inch of the greens. His Japanese companions, after about eight holes of this pathetic display of skill level, blatantly started talking to each other in Japanese. It wasn't hard for Zip to decipher that they were clowning his awful play. After nine holes Zip offered to buy a round of drinks because he felt so bad that he was forcing these guys to witness such shitty golf.

"What are you guys saying out there?" Zip asked the one guy that spoke some English.

"With apology, sir," the man replied. "But we say you terrible player."

Zip erupted laughing. "I don't speak Japanese but I knew it was along those lines."

He then proceeded to explain why he was purposely playing so poorly. How he was a coach and caddy for a pro and how he was trying to access every angle of the course in preparation to help his player in an upcoming tournament.

"This is very good to know, sir. We were quite concerned for you," the guy laughed.

After the round Zip felt so terrible he had coerced these very friendly and polite men into enduring his antics that he demanded they allow him to buy them a drink in the bar. They all laughed together and promised to follow Biggs when he played there.

After a few beers and a lovely round of sake that Harding carried, Zip was on his way home. He drove across the Bay Bridge. His notepad stocked with course tips sat on the passenger seat of his truck. He couldn't wait to share his notes with Biggs. He looked over the side of the bridge as a huge cruise ship was slowly flowing west out under the Golden Gate Bridge into a beautiful setting sun. The sun reflected off the hundreds of bright buildings and windows throughout the beautiful San Francisco skyline. He wondered where the cruise ship was headed. Why wasn't he on it? He'd often daydreamed of moving to the Philippines when Maggie went off to college. He had clients from the Philippines that said he could golf and live very well on modest means.

In this moment of tranquility, he felt things were finally going so well. His work was paying off. He was in a good place. His phone pinged. Again, it was JD. Again, with a message that pills were available. Again, he swiped the message and number away without hesitation.

It was roughly 11:00 p.m. and Zip sat at his laptop watching drone footage of Harding Park for what must have been the 100th time. His notebook of the day he played with the Japanese fellows sat next to his screen, and he frequently compared drone footage to the notes that he took on the various holes. He seemed to know every yard of the fairways. Every inch of the greens. He was as prepared as any caddy could be and he felt confident with their chances to succeed.

*How you doing?* his phone pinged with a text from Biggs. *Ready for tomorrow? I've never been so ready.*

*Yeah, I'm pumped too. Get some sleep. We've got 36 holes of good lovin' tomorrow,* Zip replied.

*I'll be ready,* Biggs answered. *I want to thank you . . .*

Zip saw the three dots blinking on his phone that signaled Biggs was in mid-thought and wanted to continue telling Zip something meaningful.

*STOP,* Zip typed quickly, cutting Biggs off before he was able to continue his meaningful text. *You don't have to say anything,* Zip continued. *We are a team and as I've told you before, you've helped me as much as I've helped you. We haven't done shit yet. Let's get out there tomorrow and show these dudes what Thomas Biggs is capable of.*

This text stopped Biggs right in his tracks. Zip had never called him by his full name. They had developed a deep friendship and love for each other.

*Good night,* Biggs simply replied.

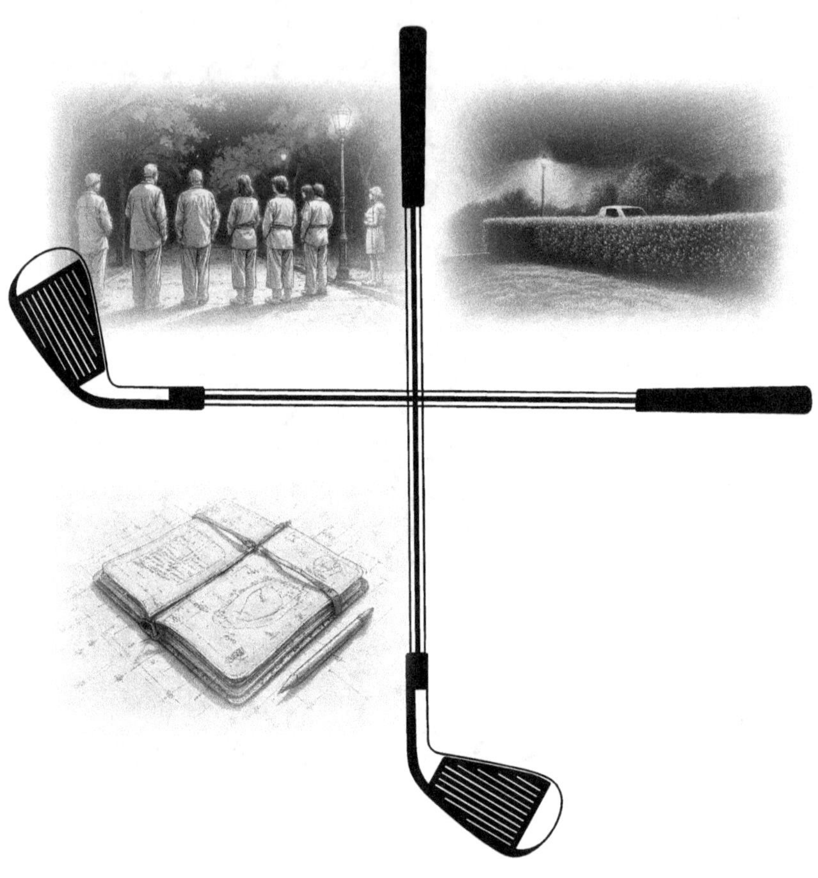

## HOLE #18

Zip went outside to take a leak in his backyard as he often did. Of course, he had bathrooms in his house, but doing his business on a tree at night reminded him of camping. It was a peaceful night in his quiet neighborhood as he gazed up into the stars. On the other side of the wooden fence that separated his yard from the street he noticed Jake's truck parked on the street with its interior light on.

"This motherfucker," Zip grumbled.

He watched Jake sitting in the car tapping on his phone. He knew immediately that Jake was trying to get Maggie's attention. He walked out to his front yard, approached Jake's window, and banged loudly on the glass, startling the shit out of a focused Jake.

"I told you to stay the fuck away!" he barked.

"But, sir, you don't understand," Jake yelled through his rolled-up window. "I just want to talk to her."

"Get the fuck outta here or I'm going to beat the living piss out of you!" Zip yelled. He again slammed his hand on Jake's driver side window. This time he almost broke the glass.

Jake rolled his window down a few inches and abruptly spit at Zip which sprayed into Zip's face. Then he quickly started his truck and pulled away as a startled Zip arched back from the vehicle to wipe the spit from his face. Jake sped up the street. Zip was livid, to say the least. He ran to his golf cart that was parked in his driveway and jumped in it, determined to catch Jake. Zip's home was at the bottom of a long circle. At the top of the circle the two roads converged into one outlet that led to a single exit. Jake had taken off up the east side of the circle which was the long way around to get to the outlet and Zip knew if he took the much shorter west side route up his street, even though he was in his slower golf cart, he could cut Jake off before he could reach the exit.

Fury raged in Zip as he slammed the gas pedal down on the golf cart. He didn't really have a plan, only that there was no fucking way he was going to let Jake get away. At the top of the circle Zip saw Jake's headlights as they both sped towards the outlet. Although Zip's cart had headlights, in his haste, he had not turned them on. Both vehicles barreled towards each other at maximum speed. Although Jake had not seen Zip's reaction, he was terrified Zip was coming after him. It was late and it was dark. Zip assumed

Jake would see him coming directly towards him and stop. But because Zip hadn't turned on his headlights, Jake did not see Zip. Nor did he stop.

Neighbors would later describe to the police that the collision they heard in the street was so violent it sounded like a train hit a stalled car on the railroad tracks. The sound ripped through the neighborhood so loudly that every person living within a five-block radius was awakened from their slumber. Jake's airbag deployed. Luckily, he was wearing his seatbelt. He would later explain to police that he never saw Zip, and that he'd never intentionally hit him, that in the darkness Zip's golf cart was invisible. Maggie had also heard the collision from her bedroom. The noise, at this time of night, in this normally quiet neighborhood, was incredibly magnified. After calling out to her father and getting no response, Maggie threw a blanket over her shoulders and walked outside to investigate.

When she saw her dad's mangled golf cart broken into two destroyed pieces of wreckage sitting on each side of the street, her chest felt a pressure that she had never experienced. Sirens blared in the distance as emergency vehicles approached the accident. But when Maggie saw her father's shoes protruding from a blanket that a neighbor who had gotten there sooner had placed over his head and body, her screams drowned out any and all sirens. Zip's body lay at least a hundred feet from where the accident occurred. He was thrown like a rag doll across the pavement. EMTs would say in their report that his skull was caved in. Their theory was that he was ejected airborne until his head met the curb that he lay next to. Blood streamed down the gutter. A neighbor that knew Maggie grabbed her as she fell on her knees next to his body. She convulsed as she shrieked and cried. It was impossible to console her. She could barely breathe as she tried to yell.

"DAD! DAD!"

Her intense grief took away her voice. The police were there taking statements. Jake was as pale as a ghost, not quite absorbing the magnitude of what had happened. He was sobbing. The neighbors all stood around in their pajamas and robes. Their hands covered their mouths. The sirens had quieted but the emergency lights from the various vehicles continued to light up the dark neighborhood and flashed off the tall trees that surrounded the street. No one had ever imagined such a tragedy could strike their peaceful community. Maggie was inconsolable.

The sun had started to rise and created some glow in the kitchen. Maggie had been seated at the stool next to the kitchen counter as the morning sun crept through the windows and brought a hint of light to the darkest night of her life. She had tried calling her mother, but her mother was asleep through the night. The heartbroken teen, who had told her neighbors that offered to stay with her that she simply wanted to be alone, sat alone in the dark throughout the night completely mortified.

By the time the morning light hit, she was all cried out. The pressure that hammered her chest was so tight she felt its grip squeezing the life out of her. Her chest heaved as she sobbed. And where tears had poured down her cheeks earlier, now there were none. Maggie had no plan. No idea what to do. How could a 16-year-old girl know anything about how to deal with the devastating blow life had just dealt. She simply sat there as the hours passed. She couldn't possibly drive to her mom's house. Her hands had not stopped trembling. Her uncontrollable chest heaves, combined with the piercingly tight grip around her heart prevented her from doing anything but just wait for her mother to wake up and read her texts to come get her.

She had first heard her Dad's phone vibrate as that first morning light crept through the small window above the sink. She presumed that was around 5:00 a.m. but she didn't look to see who was texting.  His phone sat on the edge of the counter top next to his open laptop. It was still turned on. Still displaying images of Harding Park. Zip's opened yardage book lay next to the phone. A pencil separated some of the pages that were full of notes he'd taken when he played Harding with the Japanese fellows as well as the notes he'd detailed during his drone study. Maggie looked down at a few of his final notes. They were the typical notes that read:

Keep Biggs focused.

If and when he struggles, don't let him dwell.

Keep his attitude light.

Let him know how much fun they're having, how lucky they are.

It's important, but it's JUST a game.

Rusty's waiting if he fucks up.

 Maggie had no idea what that last note meant. But at the bottom of all of it there was one last note written in black pen instead of pencil. It read:

Make Maggie proud.

Although Maggie had never met Rusty, that last note felt like the bull had just kicked her straight in her stomach. Now his phone began to vibrate again and again. As the light of the morning grew brighter and brighter, Zip's phone seemed to light up and vibrate more and more as the sun rose. Each vibration pushed the phone closer and closer to the edge of the counter until, as Maggie sat with her head in her hands, it tumbled over the edge and crashed to the floor startling her. She bent over to pick it up and saw that it was Biggs who had been trying to contact her father. She read a few of the texts from 5:00 a.m.

*You ready, my man?* it said with the strong arm emoji. *Let's do this.*

An hour or so later the texts were getting more anxious.

*Why aren't you answering? Zip? Zip? You awake?*

*You BETTER NOT be hungover,* Biggs wrote. Before finally texting,

*Where the FUCK are you? We got to get going!*

Maggie realized this was the day of the final qualifier her dad had been so excited about. She got up from the stool, straightened her frumpy clothing a bit, took a huge breath, and grabbed the keys to the truck.

The doorbell rang and within seconds Biggs aggressively swung his front door open and yelled, "Where the FUCK have you—" and stopped midsentence at the sight of Maggie standing on his porch, clearly disheveled and distraught. She extended her hand that held Zip's yardage book. Biggs instantly knew by the anguish on her face that Zip was not hungover.

"What happened?" he gently asked.

Maggie's mouth and lips were trembling as if she were freezing cold. She tried to speak but could not utter a word.

"H-h-hee's g-g-g . . ."

She tried again to say it. She tried as hard as she could to tell Biggs but she couldn't get the words "He's gone" out of her mouth. It took all of her strength just to stand there and hand him the book.

"Maggie? Are you okay? What happened? Maggie, are you okay? Where's Zip? What happened?" he peppered her with questions.

Her shock prevented any responses. By now the morning was in full swing. Birds were chirping. Lawn sprinklers were engaging. And like a wildfire the news of the accident had spread from one phone to the next. Maggie felt like she was going to collapse right there on

Biggs' porch. So, after handing him the yardage book with all of the notes, she turned and ran back to the idling truck and sped away. Biggs stood there, completely bewildered, when his phone rang.

"Hello!" he frantically answered.

"Biggs, I have to tell you something." Elliott's voice was calm and direct. "Zip was killed last night."

Before Elliot could start his next sentence, he heard a loud crashing noise. Biggs abruptly dropped his phone as what felt like a lightning bolt of shock absorbed his entire body. He blankly stared straight ahead. His view depicted a normal scene. The morning was evolving as cars were backing out of driveways headed to work, dogs were being walked, lawns mowed. But Biggs was oblivious to all of it. He just stared.

"Biggs? Biggs? BIGGS? You there?" Elliott's voice unsuccessfully called out.

Biggs' phone sat next to his feet on the porch. After a few minutes he finally reached down and picked it up.

"What happened, Elliot?" he asked.

"He was killed in an accident in the middle of the night. Some sort of a tangle with Maggie's boyfriend led to an awful wreck. I don't know too much yet. I just know he's gone. You've got the final today and—"

"Oh, fuck that," Biggs replied emotionless. "I'm out. I can't play. No fucking way. Not without Zip."

"Yeah, I don't blame you. Listen, as soon as I hear more, I'll call you."

"Okay, Elliott. Thank you."

He closed the door, meandered to his living room, and plopped on the couch. His numb demeanor continued as he sat in the outfit he had picked out for the day. He'd chosen the white shirt, white hoodie, red hat combo boldly emblazoning Rusty's head for the morning round. He figured he'd switch to the red shirt, white hat look for the afternoon. He looked down at his sleeve and thought about what Zip had told him about Street and all the people suffering with MS. It wasn't an issue if he didn't play. Who the hell was he anyway to try to bring attention to multiple sclerosis, he thought.

Suddenly his blank stare focused when he looked up and saw Jessica standing over him as opposed to being in bed.

"Why haven't you left?" she asked.

He continued his mortified gaze as if he hadn't heard a thing she said. Which he didn't.

"Hey!" she said, shaking him. "What are you doing here? You're going to be late."

"I'm not going," he finally forced out. And in a whisper that she could barely hear he said, "Zip is dead."

"Dead?" she asked. "What do you mean? Who was that that called? Who was at the front door? What do you mean dead? You two were just texting last night."

"I don't know all the details. That was Elliot. He's the guy I told you about that was sponsoring us. Said there was an accident. Said he'd call me later. So I have no idea."

Jessica sat down beside Biggs. She took the yardage book out of his hands and began to thumb through it. She didn't know what she was looking for. Perhaps there was some type of note or information Zip had left that could provide anything into the circumstances. She didn't know Zip very well and was as confused as Biggs. She perused the book simply looking for any type of clues or information that she could provide to help.

"My goodness. Look at all this info. These notes on Harding Park. He really wanted you to win," she said.

"Yeah, well, that's not going to happen," Biggs stoically replied. "There's no way I can play."

Jessica flipped through the pages and stopped abruptly on the last note. She sighed and quietly said, "Oh my God."

Biggs looked up as he heard a loud tap hit the paper of the book. He realized the tapping sound came from a large tear that had fallen from her cheek onto the page.

"Babe? You okay?" he asked.

Jessica wiped another tear from her cheek and placed the book back on his lap, keeping it open to the page that produced her tears. The page now was damp because so many tears had dropped on the paper. Zip had written a note at the bottom of the page that was now smudged by Jessica's crying. It read: Give Jessica a reason to get out of bed.

Biggs inhaled a large breath and gulped. He was barely able to hold back his own welling tears.

"I'll go with you, babe," Jessica whispered to him.

Jessica had not left the house in what seemed like forever. Biggs understood how massive this moment was.

"Jess, if you come with me, I'll fucking win it."

She stood up from the couch and looked into his eyes with a look of determination that made his heart feel like it was going to jump out of his chest.

"Give me ten minutes. Put your clubs in the car."

She took a step toward the bedroom to go get ready but abruptly stopped and turned around looking at her husband with a look of intent he hadn't seen in forever and emphatically said,

"BAT."

## HOLE #19

It was a typical early summer day at Harding Park. The course was positioned near huge cliffs that overlooked the Pacific Ocean and even though it was early June, thick fog blanketed the entire course ensuring that it would be a cold day. Many players whined and complained about being stiff in the cold or not being able to see their golf balls as they flew straight into the thick gray soup that made visibility difficult. Biggs was unfazed. He had Jessica with him. She handed him the clubs he selected. She read the notes that Zip provided in this now invaluable book. The smiles she offered him after his good shots were more rewarding than the results. More gratifying than the golf itself. Biggs also had Zip. He felt Zip's presence there with him, walking every hole in the thick fog. Biggs was in a zone. He could literally hear Zip encouraging him. Zip's infamous slogans echoed in his ears.

"The cups a fucking salad bowl," he'd hear Zip say before putts.

"There's nothing wrong with being long," he'd hear on approach shots.

"They can move the pin, but they can't move the middle of the green."

And of course, "Tap in par. Take 'em all day."

On more than a few occasions, after Biggs had put his ball in a precarious spot, he'd find notes about playing from that exact shitty location, just as Zip had purposely put himself when he played with the Japanese dudes. He was so sharp, so entirely focused, that he really hadn't kept score. Jessica was doing that. He knew he was playing well, but he just kept his head down and played the course, not the other players. He played each hole as a single entity and was only concerned with making a good score on that particular hole instead of getting too involved in his overall score or position in the field. He was also completely oblivious to all the people that were following him, and the subsequent noise they were making. After his final putt on 18 in the morning round, he looked up and broke his concentration from his play for what felt like the first time.

"Holy shit!" he exclaimed, as he looked around the outskirts of the course.

"What is it, hun?" Jess asked.

"Looks like all of Eagle Vista is here. There's Elliott, Pete . . . Shit, is that the Cal women's coach?"

He also noticed for the first time all the players from Cal's team had surrounded the green, all sporting their Cal colors as they cheered for him. The team captain, a girl named Lily, who he remembered relentlessly teasing him at the driving range, approached him and handed him a bag as he walked off the green.

"I doubt you'd want to wear this now, but we thought you needed some Cal colors." Lily giggled and hustled back to her teammates.

Biggs reached in the bag and produced a blue and gold mankini with the Cal script placed perfectly over the front crotch. He looked over at the team who were now fully enjoying their prank.

"You know what? I'm headed to change my hat and shirt and I know you guys despise any red that associates with Stanford, so I imagine a little blue and gold covering you know where could help," he joked.

"You said little, not us," Lily fired back. "Sorry, but you left that on a tee for me."

"You got to be kidding me, but I think those are a few of the cops from the cemetery?" he said, pointing to a handful of men.

"Cemetery? Mankini? A bull on your shirt? What the heck were you and Zip up to?" Jessica asked, with a smirk.

Just then LH approached. "You're in first by a stroke. You hit 9 out of 14 fairways, 26 putts, 2 sand saves, and three up and downs to save par," he rattled off in his best Rain Man impression.

"Who the hell is that?" Jess asked.

"That's Little Hitler," Biggs said flatly.

"Little what?!" she pressed.

"Hun, there's much I need to fill you in on."

Biggs indeed sat alone in first place after the first 18 holes. His swing was fluid. His putting was excellent. He'd only had to snap the rubber band on his wrist a few times to lock in his focus. He was playing amazing golf. In the men's locker room, he pulled out the red shirt to change along with the red hoodie as the fog had not let up and temperatures were still very cool. He even considered going all in with the Cal mankini but needed to hustle back out to prep for the remaining 18 holes. He stopped in front of the mirror as he exited the locker room to evaluate how he looked. He took a moment. A deep breath and he whispered, "Thank you, Zip."

In as much as he couldn't miss a shot during his morning round, the golf gods undoubtedly appeared during the first stretch of holes on the opening nine of the second round. Biggs could not find a fairway and his putter had gone ice cold. Three bogeys on the front nine had him tumbling out of first place all the way down to 6th. Only the top three Advanced to the US Open. To make matters worse, Biggs also started to hear the various moans and groans from everyone that had come out to support him. No matter how hard he tried or how hard Jessica encouraged him, he could not find the game he displayed that morning. Jessica was definitely a lift for him. But at this moment he really needed Zip.

He tried to block out what had transpired the night before but it seemed a wave of exhaustion, as strong and dense as the thick fog that covered the entire area, had finally caught Biggs. He was starting to feel completely drained. As he stood in the rough along the 14th fairway, although he was surrounded by people pulling for him and the miracle of Jessica by his side, he was exhausted. He had hit a wall. He considered withdrawing right then and there. He realized what Zip had meant to him. He so much wanted to get back on the PGA Tour. But he really wanted Zip along with him. After all, it wasn't just his dream alone. It was both of their dreams. And if Zip wasn't with him, it seemed impossible to achieve. His energy and game at this point was proving it.

"It's okay, babe. I'm so proud of you for getting to this point. I can't believe you've done what you've done today. He'd be so proud of you," Jess said, recognizing the state Biggs was in.

"I'm fucking drained, Jess. I just don't have it. I suck right now. It's over."

"I know, hun. I love you. You have nothing to hang your head about. Let's get out of here," she said in an amazingly soothing tone that reminded him why he loved her so much.

He understood that withdrawing at this point would not be a good look. But word had gotten around and nobody would have blamed him. He noticed many of the Eagle Vista folks had left. LH had been updating them on Biggs' positioning and chances of advancing which had started to dwindle. There was even some chatter about traffic going home and how they wanted to beat it, which didn't go unnoticed. Elliott wasn't leaving. Neither was the Commish. The cops were still there. As was the Cal coach and her team. Even the pessimistic LH was hanging in.

Biggs took a deep breath. Decided to reset. "Does the book say anything about this shot, babe?" Biggs asked Jessica.

He was in thick rough on the par 5 14th. A row of Harding's signature cypress trees blocked his line to the green making reaching the green in 2 impossible. Harding was not a difficult course. *If* you stayed in the fairways. The rough, however, was thick and penal which could torture even the most skilled players. Biggs had shanked his tee shot to get to this spot in the thick rough.

"Dude . . . you going to hit?" yelled one of his competitors, who by this point had become frustrated with Biggs taking so long.

"Yeah, yeah, chill, you douchebag!" he yelled back frustrated, perhaps drawing on a bit of Zip's "go fuck yourself" attitude. Which, if he was going to continue to play, he definitely needed.

"I'm sorry, babe, what's the book say about this shot?" he repeated with a sarcastic laugh because of where his ball sat.

"Believe it or not, hun, I think Zip was here. He has a note about this exact spot."

"Let me see that." Biggs laughed and grabbed the book in disbelief.

And, sure as shit, Zip had a little diagram about this shot from this location. He'd hit into this area on purpose when he played Harding a few weeks ago which undoubtedly annoyed his Japanese playing partners. Because of his shank off the tee and the fact that the hole was a par 5, Biggs still stood some 340 yards away according to the hole's total yardage.

Beneath Zip's crude diagram of the cypress trees lining the fairway and the 14th green beyond them, his note read: Trees look like they completely block green. Get 5 wood up quick. Cuts 80 yards off the distance.

A shot of adrenaline pierced through Biggs. He felt Zip's spirit in that moment. "Babe, 5 wood," he firmly requested.

"Okay, guess we're staying?" she said, handing him the club.

"Oh yeah. We're stayin'."

*THWAAAKKK!!*

Biggs hit a TOWERING ball that shot up like a rocket. His ball climbed so high that the cypress trees never threatened it. It came down out of the sky as if someone had dropped it from the Transamerica building in downtown San Francisco and made a huge thud as it stuck the green.

"Holy shit!" LH erupted.

The entire women's golf team screamed, "Go Bears!" as if they had adopted Biggs as a team member.

The ball nestled a mere five feet from the cup and Biggs calmly stroked it in for an eagle. He had gained a bit of ground but his adrenaline rush was only temporary. Now, however, he was determined to finish as he and Jess walked silently to the 15th tee. Their 33rd hole of the day.

"I feel like I've hit a wall, like Rusty steamrolled me." Biggs sighed a huge breath of exhaustion. Everything about the last 24 hours was catching up to him.

"Yeah, I'm pooped too. But you're not out of this," Jess countered.

LH had approached them on the walk between holes 14 and 15 and whispered, "Two of the top five made bogey ahead. That eagle has you on the bubble."

"Shit, really?" Biggs said, surprised. "I'm pretty gassed but let's push on."

His second shot on the par 4 15th came up short in a green side bunker. The shot was on line but too high and a last second puff of wind killed it, so it came straight down and buried into the soft sand.

"Fried egg," he said dejectedly to Jess.

He thought about the piggy bank and the coins. He hit a beautiful spinner that landed three feet beyond the cup, quickly spun back and smacked the pin directly in its center, then dropped straight into the hole.

"Well, how about that!" Jessica blurted out. "This game is crazy!"

With back-to-back eagle and birdie, Biggs erased some of his earlier woes and had  now pushed himself into the top three. The spectators that had remained on the course were now texting the EV folks that had left earlier to go drink at the bar to get their butts back out there. Word was spreading that Biggs was heating up, so many of them poured their drinks into take out cups and filed back out onto the course to follow him again. Most of them had had plenty of time to get a few drinks in them, so when they returned the atmosphere was definitely more spirited. The noise level amplified as inebriation began to conquer etiquette. This bothered Biggs very little but his playing partner, Mickey Mitchell, who was also firmly planted in the top three or four, was less than thrilled.

On the par 3 16th Mickey evaluated the joyful crowd. Agitated and annoyed, he snarled, "They with you?"

Biggs felt a bit embarrassed but was proud of his people. It was becoming evident that they'd all lost someone they'd truly loved. Cheering on Biggs and bonding as one big Eagle Vista family was helping them cope with their grief through his success. He puffed up his chest and took ownership of his new family.

"Yes, they are. They're with me."

"Well, can you get them to shut the fuck up!" he demanded.

Biggs simply smiled. He really didn't give two shits if the EV folks were bothering anyone. They'd all lost such a good friend so suddenly that if they were getting some relief by partying and cheering him on at the expense of golf etiquette, well if that's what they wanted to do, then so be it. He wasn't going to say shit to his new family. He had suppressed his emotions as much as he could. There was no gas in his tank and he knew he had very little energy left. In fact, his attention started to shift towards Jessica and how she was feeling. She hadn't been out of the house in months and he was inspired by her grit. After making workman-like pars on 16 and 17, Biggs hit a very pedestrian tee shot on 18 that, although finding the fairway, was very short.

"Jess, I'm spent. Kinda lost some distance."

"Uh, yeah, I can see that," she giggled.

Biggs and Mickey were deadlocked in a tie for the third and final spot as they both walked down the 18th fairway. The top two players were already in the clubhouse. Their positions on the leaderboard were safe. The only other players in contention were coughing up bogies so their chances to get that coveted remaining spot were toast. Had Biggs not had those amazing holes, 14 and 15, he, too, would be a slice of burnt sourdough made famous in these parts.

Mickey Mitchell, however, was a consistency machine. He was clearly perturbed by all the commotion and attention Biggs was getting and had a look in his eyes that he was going to put an end to all of this nonsense right here and now. He wasn't arrogant like Myron Pitts. But he was pissed and determined to send the drunk EV patrons back to where they came from. Someone had dropped their takeout cup during Mickey's swing on 18 tee causing him to hit a lousy shot. He brushed it off and glared at Biggs' Army as he walked off the tee box, confident that he was going to lock up third place and subsequently move on to the US Open.

"Jess, even if I could do this, how am I supposed to go to the US Open without Zip?" Biggs asked, as the two of them walked down 18.

"I honestly don't know, babe. But after lugging this bag around today there's no way I'm doing this anymore either."

"Shit, I'm so sorry. Give me that thing," Biggs said, as he grabbed the golf bag off her shoulder and threw it over his. "Give me your hand."

"You're going to hold my hand? Now?"

"You're goddamn right I am!"

They interlocked fingers and strolled down the fairway as if they were walking hand in hand on the beach. Both of them were dog tired at this point. The importance of the qualifier had completely left their minds. By the time they got to his ball, they could care less whether he was in last place or actually trying to finish third. Both Biggs and Mickey, after their mediocre tee shots, had approximately 170 yards to the pin. When they got to his ball, Jessica looked at Biggs. He had tears flowing down his face.

"You've played your heart out, Thomas. It's okay. What you've endured emotionally let alone mentally and physically today would—" Jessica abruptly stopped talking mid-sentence. Her expression changed as if she had suddenly seen a ghost behind her husband.

Biggs looked up at Jessica confused at her sudden silence. He wiped the tears away with his gloved hand and turned to look in the direction his now exasperated wife was looking.

"HOLEEEY SHIT," he said under his breath.

Behind him, in a tree-lined section just off the fairway where there were no other spectators, under a beautiful cypress tree, was a lone figure wearing a dark hoodie.

It was Maggie.

A tingling sensation shot up Biggs' spine like nothing he'd ever felt before. He was flabbergasted to see her. They looked at each other and Maggie gave him a simple nod of encouragement. The connection they felt in that moment, on that golf course, felt supernatural. Instantly, a shot of adrenaline and energy pulsated through Biggs' body.

"What's the fucking book say?" he demanded, with a fierce level of confidence that Jess hadn't heard in at least the last 4 or 5 holes.

Jessica gathered herself and flipped open the yardage book to the 18th hole. "You're not going to believe this. But I think he was standing right here too. Zip's note says if the pin is middle green, if it's cold, to play a longer club. But if it's warm, also play the longer club. He wrote there's a funnel at the top of the green that can't be seen from the fairway. Said to hit it long and it'll catch it and roll to the hole."

Mickey was away by a few feet and played first. He hit a perfect 7 iron that majestically tracked towards the green. He spun his club and walked intently after he struck it.

"That's money," he yelled.

His reaction was a tad arrogant as golf etiquette standards go. But at this point, with all the shenanigans he'd heard from Biggs' gallery, he cared less. His ball sailed directly towards the green but in the cool fog suddenly came crashing down some 20 yards short, and disappeared into the thick rough that surrounded the green. Mickey just stood there in disbelief. He even looked at the number on the bottom of his club to verify that he'd hit the correct distance. He had nutted that ball square but somehow it didn't travel the distance he surely assumed that it would. Par was still in play but with the ball buried in thick grass well off the green and nowhere near the pin, saving par was going to be a difficult, if not impossible, challenge.

"DAMMIT! That's it! I have had it! This is bullshit!" he yelled and glared at the gallery looking for an excuse for his shot.

"Can you people ever just shut the FUCK UP?!" he screamed at them.

Biggs calmly looked at Jess. Then gazed to his left over at Maggie.

"Funnel, huh?"

"That's what it says," she quipped.

Biggs addressed the ball and then stepped back for a moment. He looked at all of the folks that suddenly were now quiet and feeling a bit embarrassed after being lambasted by Mickey. Biggs raised both his hands to the sky and motioned for them to make noise. They obliged him by providing huge roars of encouragement to which he flapped his arms harder asking them to be even louder. And on cue, for the first time all day, the thick fog began to quickly dissipate as the warm, bright sun emerged over the entire course. On such foggy coastal days, when the fog lifts, it disappears at breakneck speed. Suddenly Biggs was standing over his shot with the warm sun blazing down on his neck and shoulders. He considered using a different club because of the instantaneous temperature change.

"If it's warm, play the longer club," Jessica reminded him. For a moment, he initially thought the 6 iron he purely flushed off his clubface was hit too well, and too long.

The ball soared into the new sunlight that Biggs was convinced somehow Zip had created. Biggs imagined Zip's spirit riding on the ball as it seemingly floated through the blue sky. He didn't spin his club. He didn't arrogantly hype the moment.

He simply looked at Jess and said, "Let's go home."

The crowd collectively let out a sustained disappointed groan when his ball plunged from the sky onto the green but nowhere near the pin. But then, like clockwork, as if Zip's spirit inhaled a huge breath and blew hard against it, the ball trickled into the funnel and slowly crawled down it until the ball gently stopped an inch from the cup. The crowd erupted with a deafening roar.

Biggs looked to the heavens, to his friend and mentor, and calmly announced, "Tap in birdie. Take 'em all day!"

My friend pictured on my right is the true definition of the word.
He didn't inspire me to write this story but if I can bring any
amount of attention to his condition that encapsulates far too
many awful adjectives to describe, I will be forever indebted.
This photo was taken at the 1998 US Open in San Francisco.
Soberly, it demonstrates the young man he was with the per-
ceived future ahead. But we all know, life has its plan.
I would also like to acknowledge my Bros at Crow Canyon for
our brotherhood and providing endless content.
I would like to thank the poor stationary bike at the gym whose
pedals I broke twice while spending hours typing this story into
my iPhone 7 Notes (Apple does not define me) proving that one
could create art while working out.
I also need to acknowledge my Mom. A fantastic English teacher
that provided my foundation and most importantly, confidence
to write. Never a finer person, mentor, or mother. For the nights
we butted heads at the kitchen table as you proofread my
school papers only to throw the papers in the air while yelling
"Why do you even ask me for help?! You fucking write it the way
you want it then!" I am wholeheartedly grateful.
And of course to my Tinkers, Punkers, Mimi... you saved my
bacon kid. follow your dreams. SAT!
Lastly, for all of us that get frustrated missing a 3-foot birdie,
remember,
Tap in par Take em all day

*Proceeds from your generous purchase of Rabbit Earz will support people who are cruelly afflicted with Multiple Sclerosis. Living with MS is costly in so many ways. We wish to generate funds for counseling, physical therapy, mobility aid, orthotic care, nursing, and basically ANY need someone struggling with this horrible disease would have to help improve their lives.*

*Please jump on board our grassroots effort. Reach out to me directly on one of the various social media platforms or email below to purchase a copy(s) for yourself, friends, family. Provide an address and, if you like, a personalized note you'd like me to write in your signed copy. Each copy is $20 plus postage.*

*Feel free to leave a review which can be posted on our social media or possibly in future prints.*

**"Read this book in your warm bed rather than having a bucket of ice dumped on your head!"**

Rabbitearzbook@gmail.com
Instagram @Rabbitearzbook
Facebook Rabbitearzbook
Venmo @Rabbitearzbook
PayPal.me/ Rabbitearzbook

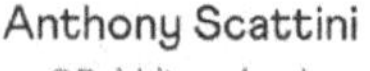